RED SKY

A POST-APOCALYPTIC NOVEL

KELLEE L. GREENE

BOOKS BY KELLEE L. GREENE

Falling Darkness Series

Unholy - Book 1

Uprising - Book 2

Hunted - Book 3

Ravaged Land Series

Ravaged Land -Book 1

Finding Home - Book 2

Crashing Down - Book 3

Running Away - Book 4

Escaping Fear - Book 5

Fighting Back - Book 6

Ravaged Land: Divided Series

The Last Disaster - Book 1

The Last Remnants - Book 2

The Last Struggle - Book 3

The Island Series

ONE

There hadn't been any warnings leading up to the catastrophe, at least none that normal people like myself had been given. I hadn't been prepared for the day it happened. But then again, no one had been.

I shot up in my bed bending forward at my waist, gasping for air. My fingertips gripped the floral bedspread my grandma had bought three years ago for my twenty-second birthday.

Sweat dripped down the sides of my face, landing on the pretty purple and pink carnation print. The room spun as if I was on a merry-go-round.

My heart raced as I tried to suck oxygen deep into my lungs. It felt as though my upper body had been stuffed with cotton, and my throat was being sewn shut.

I swung my legs over the side of the bed, placing my feet firmly on the floor. My fingers dug into the side of the bed as if I was afraid the swirling motion was going to throw me off the mattress and onto the floor. I lowered my head, taking slow breaths in a desperate attempt to calm myself.

A panic attack? It wouldn't be the first one I'd had, and it would unlikely be the last. But somehow this was different.

I couldn't remember my dream, but it must have been pretty terrible to send my body into the hell I was currently inside of. It must have been a nightmare, so bad my body was refusing to let me recall it.

The dreams had seemed to be happening more and more, especially with my ever-increasing bouts of insomnia over the last few weeks. And I knew I shouldn't have watched the news before bed. That always puts my mind in dark places.

Ever since I'd lost my job, things had been rough. I wasn't sure how I was going to pay my next month's rent, not to mention my dinner had been junk off of the dollar menu. The last thing I wanted to do was to have to call my grandma and beg her for money... again.

I drew in a shaky breath as I looked over at my phone on the nightstand. The light was blinking, but as I was about to reach over and check the message, a sharp pain shot through my gut. It felt like my stomach was being squeezed in a vice. Sourness bubbled up in my esophagus, and my eyes widened.

At first, I tried to swallow, hoping to force everything back down, but my body was refusing to comply. I covered my mouth with my hand and tried to breathe, but it felt like I was going to explode.

I charged across the bedroom floor and stumbled my way into the bathroom. There hadn't even been enough time to put the light on before I bent at the middle and held my own hair back. My stomach lurched and emptied itself into the white porcelain bowl.

The coolness of the tile floor on my feet was a welcomed relief. I was tempted to lay down next to the toilet.

"Ugh," I groaned as I placed my palms on the counter and leaned over the sink. I turned on the faucet and splashed water on my face. My eyes shifted up, and I caught the reflection of my pale skin that almost seemed to be glowing in the dark.

I stepped out of the bathroom and crossed the floor, making my way into the tiny kitchen of my small apartment. The worn carpet felt rough against the bottoms of my bare feet.

I reached inside the fridge and pulled out a bottle of cold water. My fingers shook as I unscrewed the cap. I swallowed down a big gulp of water in an attempt to wash down the putrid taste that felt stuck to the back of my throat.

My clothing clung to my body as more beads of sweat accumulated on my forehead. I placed the back of my hand to my head to feel if I had a fever, but the only thing I could tell was that I was so hot that I was sweating.

The air in my apartment felt thick, like a fog caused by dense summer humidity. Somehow, I was managing to take in breaths even though with the pressure in my chest, it was a bit of a challenge.

I leaned back against the wall, pressing the bottle of water to my forehead and noticed through the curtains that the sun was starting to come up. Great. Of course, it felt as though I hadn't slept at all.

The glow around the edges of the curtains seemed different from usual. It was brighter... more orange. Even though I probably should have crawled back into bed to get more rest, I walked over the window and pulled back the curtain.

When I saw the red color that covered the entire

sky, my mouth dropped wide open. Every inch was a shade of red much like blood, and unlike anything I'd ever seen before.

"What the hell?" I said, looking at the trees in the yard. Was I still dreaming? The leaves and grasses were varying shades of dark red, colored by the unusual sky.

I drew in a breath that pinched my lungs as I tried to make sense of what I was seeing. The air got stuck in my throat forcing me to release a harsh, painful cough.

Something wasn't right.

In fact, a lot of things didn't seem right.

I reached over for the remote to check the TV and it felt like a volcano was about to erupt inside my stomach. The local news station was showing nothing but rainbow-colored lines up and down the screen.

"What the...."

As I was about to flip to the next channel, a severe, ice-cold shiver ran down my spine. My bones felt cold even though my apartment felt like it was preheating to cook a pizza.

My fingers trembled as I checked the next channel, and then the one after that. Both showing the same rainbow-colored stripes. Maybe if I would

5

have had cable, there would have been something useful.

I remembered my phone in the other room. With my arms wrapped around my stomach as if I was holding myself together, I dashed into my bedroom. My fingers shaking as I picked the phone up off of the nightstand.

The redness from the sky peeked through the blinds making red stripes across the wall. It looked as though my bedroom had been turned into a dark-room for developing photos.

I pressed the button on my phone, instantly noticing that I only had three percent battery remaining. There were two text messages.

The first was from my friend Molly asking where I was and why I wasn't answering my phone. She should have known I'd be trying to sleep in the middle of the night.

The second message was from my brother Nick asking me to call him which was followed by three exclamation points.

My brother?

I looked toward the window and then back at my phone. It had been at least two years since I'd talked to my brother. Maybe even longer.

The last time I had talked to him had been at our mother's funeral.

After Nick was kicked off the police force, he spiraled out of control in a way no one could have seen coming. It was much different from the way I was currently spiraling.

Nick had gotten into drugs, he'd had an affair with a prostitute which led to a divorce, and so much more. His coin had completely flipped whereas I was still sitting on the edge of my coin trying to keep in balanced.

I reached down toward the plug to charge my phone. Even though I didn't want to, I should at least text him back.

Just as I inserted the plug, the phone shut off and the familiar hum of electricity in my apartment disappeared. There was no sound coming from the TV in the other room, just an eerie silence hanging in the air.

Before I could even press the button to turn my phone back on to check the internet for information, my stomach sloshed like a broken wash machine on spin cycle. There was no way I was going to make it to the bathroom.

I dropped to my knees and threw up in the small trash bin next to my nightstand.

After I finished, I hovered over it for a few minutes before I could gather up enough energy to pull myself back into the bed. I rested my head down on my squishy pillow and closed my eyes, begging my stomach to settle.

Nick could wait. So could Molly.

It took several minutes before my body relaxed and I was brave enough to move. I raised my hand up to my forehead and wiped the sweat away.

My eyelids felt heavy, but I wanted to check my phone. There had to be something about the red sky, it was too odd not for some news site to be reporting on it.

I clicked the button to turn it on, but nothing happened. The electricity was out... my phone was dead... and the sky was the color of a vampire's cocktail. Something was most definitely wrong.

What a great time to get sick. But none of it really mattered. I was far too ill to worry about the phone or the electricity. Hell, I was far too sick to even worry about the bizarre red sky.

As for the electricity, I probably hadn't paid the bill. And without power, I wouldn't be able to charge my phone to call the electric company.

Wonderful.

My pillow, t-shirt, and shorts were drenched in

sweat, but all I could do was lay there staring at the wall hoping to God I didn't throw up again. There couldn't have even been anything left inside of me.

I shivered as the world outside brightened. The sun was rising higher, but whatever was causing the redness was still out there.

My body wouldn't stop shaking. I couldn't even remember the last time I'd felt this sick. Maybe never. If I could have afforded a doctor bill, this maybe would have been the time to go see one.

I think I started to dream, or maybe I was hallucinating, but my mother was suddenly alive. She was inside my apartment, in the kitchen, making me chicken noodle soup from scratch. Deep down inside, I knew she wasn't really there. It wasn't possible no matter how badly I wanted to see her again.

Maybe I'd died. But what kind of afterlife would it be if I continued to feel so sick?

Her footsteps tapped softly against the old linoleum floor. I saw her shadow through the door as she moved from one side of the kitchen to the other.

"It's almost ready, sweetheart," she called out to me. Her voice soothed me more than the chicken soup ever would.

I wanted to respond... to see her close up... to hug

her, but my voice wouldn't work. I couldn't beg her to come into the bedroom before I woke.

My eyelids fluttered rapidly, bringing me back into my now red bedroom. For a moment, I wasn't sure what was real and what was a dream. I listened for her footsteps, but the apartment was silent. Too silent. Hauntingly silent.

As I stared at the red lines on the wall, I heard a woman scream somewhere outside. It was far away, but I could still tell it had been there. Moments later, several pops from a gun erupted, and my body shuddered with each one.

Guns? Maybe I was still dreaming.

When there was a sharp knock at the door, my eyes widened. It was definitely real. The world I could reach out and touch wasn't the dream.

How long had I been asleep for?

"Gwen!" the voice called loudly before urgently pounding three more times. "Hurry up! Let me in!"

TWO

I wobbled as I got myself onto my feet. Somehow, I managed to walk through my apartment to the door. Whoever was out there didn't seem like would stop pounding until I did.

"Hang on," I muttered, but surely, they wouldn't be able to hear my weak voice through the door. And I wasn't even sure if I had wanted them to.

I twisted the deadbolt and unlocked the door just barely stepping to the side as the guy from down the hall pushed past me and closed my door. He looked as though he was just as pale and sweaty as I was.

"You should look before letting someone inside," Jamie said looking me up and down. "You're lucky it was me and not some creepy rapist."

"How do you know I didn't?"

"Did you?"

I shook my head.

I didn't know Jamie all that well, only from a few random chats when we'd pass each other in the hallway. He could have been a creep for all I knew, but he seemed like a nice, normal guy for the times I had talked with him.

What I did know about Jamie was that he worked for a package delivery company and that he brewed his own coffee. He had his own disposable cups that he carried on his way to work. I also knew that he left early in the morning for his job and that he was extremely good-looking. It didn't seem as though he was aware of that fact, but I definitely was.

His brilliant blue eyes looked purple-ish in the red glow of my apartment.

"Can I help you with something?" I asked, my voice groggy. I tried to hide the fact that I kind of wished he wasn't seeing me at my worst.

In all the time I'd lived in the same apartment building as Jamie Bennett, not once had he knocked on my door. He wasn't the type to borrow a cup of sugar from a neighbor. In fact, if I had to guess, I'd wager he drank his coffee black.

His mouth dropped open as he stared into my

eyes. He slowly cocked his head to the side. "Did you not see what's going on out there?"

"I saw, but then I got really sick, and honestly that's mostly all I've been thinking about so far this morning," I said, placing my hand on the wall to help steady myself. My legs were weak, and they were starting to shake. If I didn't sit down soon, I'd probably crash to the floor.

"Yeah, you look far worse than I do," Jamie said.

"Thanks? I hope that's not all you stopped by to tell me."

Jamie shook his head. "That came out much worse than I intended. Anyway, something is going on out there. Something happened. There was some kind of... attack."

"An attack?" I questioned, my voice flat. It was almost as if it were the first time I'd ever heard the word.

"Yeah before the power went out, I caught a quick warning one of the news channels just as I was stepping out of the shower." Jamie ran his hand through his wavy hair. "They said it was some kind of attack, stay indoors, wait for more information, but then the station went out."

Jamie started pacing, twisting his fingers as he moved quickly back and forth. He stopped abruptly and wiped the back of his hand across his brow.

"It was still dark when I first woke, but it wasn't long after that I passed out. I don't know what's going on out there, but I do know that you are the first person to answer their door," he said.

"Maybe everyone is still asleep," I said placing my hand on my stomach. "Ugh, I'm so sorry, but I think I'm going to be sick again."

"This is going to sound absolutely crazy, but I think whatever it is... I think it's in the air. Some kind of chemical, or poison."

"What makes you think that?" I asked.

"The color of the sky."

I winced as my knees threatened to give out. Jamie dashed over to me and grabbed my elbow. He carried most of my weight as he helped me to the sofa.

"What about your phone?" I asked lowering my head down on a small square pillow with a giant lobster stitched on it. The red colored thread matched the color peeking out from behind my curtains.

Jamie sighed. "I tried calling a couple people before my phone stopped working. No one answers their phone at four in the morning."

"It doesn't work at all?" I asked. What were the odds we were both out of battery?

"Won't even turn on. How about yours?"

"Same."

Jamie looked toward the window as he crossed his arms. "I don't know what to do about any of this."

"There isn't anything we can do, is there?" My voice was embarrassingly whiny. "Oh, God, if I move I'm going to throw up again."

"Well then, don't move." Jamie flashed me a weak smile.

"I wasn't planning on it." I let out a heavy sigh and closed my eyes, mentally begging my stomach to settle itself. I didn't want my attractive neighbor to witness me vomiting on his first visit. "Were you this sick too?"

Jamie swallowed. "Sick enough. Still feel kind of terrible, but I stopped throwing up about an hour ago. Otherwise, I probably wouldn't have been able to leave my apartment."

"Any other symptoms?"

"Looks to be the same as what you're going through. Chills, fever, sweating profusely, stomach pain, and vomiting."

"Sounds about right. At any point did you feel

like you might die?" I asked touching my chest as I remembered the squeezing I'd first felt in my lungs.

Jamie's head slowly bobbed up and down. "It was awful when I first woke. I thought I was being choked to death."

My stomach clenched, and I exhaled slowly between my lips.

"And now I'm here, in your apartment because I freaked out. I don't know what the fuck to do about any of this. Shit," Jamie said combing his fingers through his hair. "Maybe I'm overreacting."

"Do you think there's someone out there that knows what happened?" I asked.

"No idea. With the sky that color I'm not sure I want to venture out there to find out. I keep hearing the news reporters voice repeating in the back of my head to stay indoors." Jamie looked toward the window. "Seems like good advice."

I wanted to nod, but I wasn't sure it was a good idea to move my head. "Would you mind grabbing me that bottle of water off the counter?"

Jamie was in front of me unscrewing the cap in a matter of seconds. Even though he barely knew me, he seemed concerned. He helped me raise my head so that I could take a small sip.

"Guess I'm not going to work today," he said with a chuckle. "Can't even call in sick."

"I haven't been doing that for a while," I said resting my head back down on the pillow.

"Doing what?"

"Going to work."

Jamie screwed the cap back on the bottle and set it down on the coffee table. "Sorry to hear that. Maybe I can hook you up with something down at...," his voice faded away into nothing. "What the hell am I talking about? A possible attack on us, and I'm talking about helping you find a new job."

"No, it's fine. I appreciate it. And when I'm feeling better, and this is all over, I'll appreciate it even more. But for now, my only goal is to not throw up again especially not while I have company."

"Don't let my being here stop you," Jamie said with a smile. "I threw up my share, and honestly with each one, I think I felt a little better."

"Then I might need to throw up a lot."

Jamie raised a brow. "I'll hold your hair back."

"Let's hope it doesn't come to that," I said unable to stop the small smile from curling the ends of my lips.

"Do you mind if I stay here for a while? You

know to keep you company, and definitely not because I was freaking out on my own."

I swallowed and let my eyes close. "I don't mind."

Oddly I didn't. Jamie's company actually made me feel a little better, but if I had to throw up again, I wasn't going to take him up on his offer to hold my hair back. I didn't know him well enough for that.

"It's weird," I said without opening my eyes.

"What's weird?" Jamie said sounding overly interested in what I was going to say. He was about to be disappointed.

"My brother sent me a text telling me to call him. And before you ask why that's weird, it's because I haven't talked to my brother in a couple years." I squeezed my eyes shut as my stomach gurgled.

Jamie folded his hands into his lap. "Interesting. Are you worried about him?"

"Yes, and no. He used to be a cop, but it's unusual he messaged. I'm surprised he still had my number."

"When was the message from?" Jamie asked.

"This morning."

Jamie nodded. "Where does he live?"

"Just outside of the city."

"You live this close, and you haven't talked to him in years?"

I chewed my lip for a moment. "It's complicated."

"Sibling rivalry?"

"Not really."

"Well, hopefully, that means he's okay," Jamie said. I stared at him. "You know, because he messaged."

I swallowed hard. "Does that mean you think people aren't okay?"

There hadn't been much color in Jamie's face but what had been there washed away. His eyes shifted down toward his feet, and there was no need for him to answer me.

Jamie cleared his throat and pointed his chin toward the bottle of water. "Need another drink?"

"Yes, please," I said.

"Here you go," Jamie said softly as he helped me take a drink. I could smell the fresh, brisk scent from the soap he'd used in the shower.

If I thought I'd be able to keep myself up long enough, I would have forced myself to take a shower. Maybe if I could have cleaned up, I would have started to feel better.

I watched Jamie as he walked over to the

window. He peeked out between the curtains staring out at the same backyard he'd be able to see from the window in his apartment.

My eyelids started to close. Each blink lasted longer than the last. I wasn't sure, but I may have dozed off because when I opened my eyes again, Jamie was sitting in the chair.

The bubbling in my stomach seemed to have ceased, and I wasn't sweating nearly as much. Perhaps whatever had been affecting me was subsiding.

I pushed myself up, leaning my back against the armrest. Even if I was starting to feel better, I was still terribly weak.

"How are you feeling?" Jamie asked leaning forward in the chair. "Need some water?"

I did, but I felt capable of getting it myself. Just as I reached over to grab my bottle of water, something slammed into the wall near my front door.

My eyes darted over, instantly meeting Jamie's. His voice was softer than a cotton ball. "Expecting someone?"

I shook my head.

There was another heavy thud, followed by a groan. "Help me!"

THREE

Neither Jamie nor I moved. Our eyes were locked in an intense, anxious stare.

"Anyone in there? Please! I need help!" the voice called out. Seconds later, sounds of scraping moved across the wall, stopping when they pounded on the door next to mine. "Help!" they called again. "Please! Someone!"

"Should we help?" Jamie asked.

My eyes widened. "I have no idea. I can barely help myself."

"It's your apartment. Your call." Jamie shrugged.

I stared at him for a long moment before swinging my legs over the side of my sofa. The muscles in my calves tensed as if I was on the verge of getting a charley horse.

"What are you doing?" Jamie asked as I stood. He was in a crouched position somewhere between sitting and standing. It looked like he was ready to launch himself forward if I couldn't hold myself up.

"I'm going to take a peek."

"Want me to do it?"

I pressed my lips together. "It's fine. You're right, it's my place. But I doubt there is anything I can do to help."

My steps toward the door were cautious and careful. Whoever was out there was at least two doors down by the time I stepped in front of my door. I peeked out of the peephole, but there wasn't anyone in the hall that I could see.

The door squeaked as I slowly pulled it open, my fingertips were white as I held it in place. I drew in a breath as I ducked my head out.

"Help me!" the woman screeched in my face as they popped out from around my other side.

The woman reached out for me, but I managed to pull back just out of her reach. She was dripping sweat, her hair tangled in huge knots on top of her head.

"What's happening to me?" she asked.

I shook my head, unable to stop staring at the red blisters on her face that seemed to be popping and oozing before my eyes. As I opened my mouth, Jamie slammed the door shut and quickly flipped the locks into place.

"Holy shit," Jamie said practically panting as his eyes bulged out of their sockets.

The woman outside the door pounded with both fists. She screamed obscenities for at least a minute before she broke down in tears.

"Go back to your apartment," Jamie shouted through the door. "Stay indoors."

"Fuck you!" the woman shouted before kicking the door. "I'm dying!"

"Sorry," I called out. "I'm sick too."

Her sobbing turned into maniacal laughs that sent a chilly shiver down my spine.

"You don't know what sick is," the woman kicked the door again before the air was filled with a heavy thud.

I looked out of the peephole at the woman lying on the ground outside my door. Her body was convulsing, and blood was pouring out of her nose. White foam bubbled out of her mouth and dripped onto the carpet.

"Jesus!" I said taking a quick step back.

Jamie stepped forward and stared out of the

peephole. His mouth hung open, horrified at the sigh outside my apartment door.

He took a quick step back with his palms out. His head slowly turned toward the window. "We can't go out there."

I swallowed hard, my eyes moved over my skin looking for blisters and lesions that weren't there ten seconds ago. Did the woman contaminate me? Had she touched me? I couldn't remember, but thankfully my skin was the same as it always had been.

"I need a shower," I said holding my arms out at my sides as if I were afraid to let them touch my body.

"Me too." Jamie caught my eyes for a second. He scratched the back of my neck. "Not like that. I mean, by myself. Never mind."

"I didn't think, um, yeah," I said, crossing my arms in front of my chest awkwardly. "Anyway, I'll be back in a few minutes. Don't let anyone in."

Jamie snorted. "You can bet on that."

I grabbed a set of fresh clothing from my room before locking myself in my bathroom. The light that came in through the small window stained the walls bright red.

I turned on the water, undressed and lowered myself into the tub, letting the water rain down on me. I grabbed the bar of soap at the edge of the tub and scrubbed it all over my skin. Twice.

There was a part of me that wanted to stay in the tub. I felt safer. Hidden. Outside of the tub was sickness and confusion.

I forced myself to stand up and dry off. Hearing Jamie pacing in the other room reminded me I couldn't hide out forever.

I brushed my still wet hair and straightened my slightly wrinkled t-shirt before letting out a heavy sigh. The shower had definitely helped, but my body still felt weak.

Jamie's eyes darted over to me when I stepped out of the bathroom. They lingered for a moment before he held up a water bottle.

"I borrowed one, I hope that's okay," he said.

"No problem. I'm sorry, I didn't offer you something to drink earlier. I was a bit off my game."

Jamie cocked his head to the side. "Does that mean you're feeling better?"

"I am," I said, as I walked into the kitchen and pulled down a box of cereal bars. "Would you like one?"

"Sure," Jamie said.

I pulled out a bar and tossed it to him. He caught

25

it with one hand, ripped it open and ate half of the bar in one bite.

"Hungry?" I asked.

"Yes, and no," Jamie said, and I nodded, understanding completely. He popped the last half into his mouth. "We'll find out soon if it stays down."

It was weird having Jamie inside my apartment, but at the same time, I was glad he was there with me. Unfortunately, neither of us had any idea what was going on outside that was putting us in this interesting predicament.

If it was some kind of attack when would it be safe to go outside? Eventually, I'd run out of food, and we would need to leave. Would someone come for us? The phone didn't work so we couldn't call anyone, and without electricity, we couldn't check the TV or internet for information. Not know what was going on was beyond frustrating. It was frightening. Terrifying.

One of the last things Jamie had heard before the power went out was to stay inside. That was the only thing we could do as far as I was concerned. With the sky bleeding, out there was one of the last places I wanted to be.

I wondered about my brother. Did he know what

was going on? Was he okay? Was that why he tried reaching out to me after all this time?

For all I knew, the same thing that had happened to the woman outside of my apartment had happened to him too. Maybe he'd called to say good-bye, or that he was sorry for the hell, he'd put our family through.

"If that was some kind of poison, a chemical, or whatever, do you think since we're sitting here that we somehow managed to survive it?" I asked turning to the side, so I didn't have to look into Jamie's eyes. "Or do you think it could still happen to us?"

I was unable to stop my eyes from fixing on the door. It was almost as though I had x-ray vision and I could see the woman lying on the ground oozing and dripping blood all over the hallway carpet like a fountain.

"I can't even guess," Jamie said. "But I do think it's best if we just stay inside. They'll let us know when it's safe to go out again."

"Exactly who will let us know?"

"I don't know." Jamie shrugged. "Whoever is still out there. There has to be someone, right? The police... or maybe the military."

"Yeah, maybe," I said not feeling any amount of confidence in my words. If whoever was out there had things figured out, they would have been able to warn us before it had gotten to this point. I combed my finger through my hair as the reality of the situation set in. "Jesus. What are we going to do?"

Jamie stared at my shaking fingers before I could hide them behind my back.

"That lady," I said as visions of her popped into my head. "The way she died... that was... that was just—"

"Horrific? Try not to think about it."

"How can I not?"

Jamie swallowed. "There wasn't anything we could have done for her. Besides, I'm the one that closed the door."

I let out a heavy sigh as I walked past him and into my living room, lowering myself down onto the sofa. My legs were still too weak from whatever I'd gone through.

"I hope you're right," I said shaking my head. "Of course, you have to be right. But what do we do in the meantime? You're welcome to stay as long as you'd like."

It was crazy to offer, but I was scared out of my mind, and I didn't want to be alone.

"Thanks, I'd like that." Jamie smiled as he sat

down in the chair. "You must think I'm the biggest wuss in the world."

I narrowed my eyes at him. "What? Of course not. Why would you say that?"

"Because I'm too scared to go back to my own apartment." Jamie flashed me a bright grin that was almost comforting. In fact, it would have been if his skin tone hadn't been tinted red.

"If it makes you feel better, I'd be totally freaking out if you weren't here."

Jamie chuckled. "It doesn't, really." He sucked in a deep breath, and with it, his eyes darkened. "This is just beyond anything I could have ever imagined. I mean, I never really thought anything like this would happen."

"Me either."

"Do you know anyone else in the building?" Jamie asked.

I shook my head. "This is going to sound pathetic, but you're the only one I know."

"Yeah, you kept to yourself, didn't you?"

"That'll be on my headstone." I swallowed and tasted a bit of that sourness I'd experienced earlier. "Which might happen sooner than expected."

"Don't say that."

"Sorry." I pressed my lips together and twisted my fingers. "Did you know anyone else?"

Jamie shook his head. "Not really. There was a guy on the first floor I met a few times, and another woman I knew a little."

"Do you have any family that lives in the city?" I asked.

"No, other side of the country." Jamie looked down at his hands. "Hopefully, they're all okay."

I nodded, not knowing what words I could offer that might help ease his worries. If he was worried. I couldn't tell by his blank expression. Maybe he didn't know how to feel considering we had no idea what our own futures held.

We sat there in silence. Both seemingly lost in our own thoughts. I was thinking about my brother even though I wasn't sure why. He'd separated long ago from the family, making it clear he hadn't wanted anything to do with us.

But why had he called? Did he know what was going on? Maybe he'd been trying to check on me, to make sure I was okay, but I hadn't answered.

If we ever got to leave, I'd go to his place and check for him. Although I wasn't sure why I even cared since he hadn't given a shit about me the last couple years.

He'd cared enough to call. That had to count for something.

"Did you hear that?" Jamie asked breaking the silence with a sharp whisper.

I shook my head.

Jamie stood up, his shoulders moving up and down as he stared at the door. "Someone's out there."

FOUR

Jamie grabbed my hand and led me into my bedroom. He stood in front of me and pressed his index finger to his lips.

I could hear whoever was out there knock on the door at the end of the hall... Jamie's door. His body was rigid as he listened.

"Any survivors in there?" the voice called out after knocking on another door. It wouldn't be long before they were knocking at my door.

I could hear the hallway floorboards creak as they came closer. Everything was so quiet I could hear their voices through the wall.

"Oh my God, Mrs. Philips," a woman said. "She was such a nice lady."

Even though I knew it was coming, my body jerked when they knocked on my door.

"Anyone in there?" a man's voice bellowed. "We're looking for survivors!"

I turned to Jamie. "Maybe they know what happened. Maybe it's help."

"Maybe, but I remember what happened last time we opened the door."

"I'll look, stay here," I said touching his shoulder as I stepped around his tensed body.

He narrowed his eyes at me for a moment before shaking his head. I could feel him following close behind me.

"I can hear you in there," the man's voice called out, and I froze. "We're not sick."

I looked at Jamie over my shoulder, but all he could offer me was half of a shrug.

"We just want to talk," the voice said, followed by three soft taps at the door.

I drew in a breath and walked over to the door. Out of the peephole, I could see three of them standing there, alternating between staring at the door and nervously looking up and down the hallway.

"They don't look sick," I said. "At least not any more than you or I."

"Okay," Jamie said taking a step back. He stepped into the kitchen and grabbed my broom. "Just in case."

My eyebrows squeezed tightly together. "I have steak knives."

"Let's hope it won't come to that," Jamie said, and I wasn't sure if he was joking.

My fingers trembled as I turned the lock. I wasn't even sure why I felt so afraid, after all, we were all going through the same thing.

I opened the door, just a crack, setting my foot on the other side locking it into place. The man and two women stared at me with wide eyes.

"What can I do for you?" I asked working to keep my voice steady.

"We're going around the building, checking for survivors," the man said. "So far, it's just us. Well and you."

He couldn't see Jamie from where he stood, and I didn't bother to mention he was there.

"I'm Bronx, and this is Blair and Maggie."

"Hi," the one he'd pointed to when he'd said Blair raised her hand.

She was a bombshell. The woman seemed doll-like with her perfectly styled platinum blond hair.

The other woman stayed tucked away behind

Bronx. Her hair was not quite shoulder length, hot chocolate brown, and disheveled. There was so much fear and uncertainty in her eyes it made me uncomfortable.

Bronx was a broad-shouldered man, carrying himself with a confidence I couldn't even comprehend. His dark eyes smiled at me.

"Are you here alone?" he asked. My eyes shifted. "If you'd like, you can come with us."

"I'm fine here," I said answering quickly.

"We all live here," Bronx said as if he could tell I was uneasy. "In this building."

I studied their faces, but I wasn't sure I'd ever seen any of them before. That, of course, wasn't their fault it was mine for only leaving when I had to.

"Can we come in? We just want to talk," Bronx said.

I pressed my lips together, my shoulders sinking slightly as I stepped to the side. Their eyes all seemed to settle on Jamie at the same time.

"Oh," Bronx said looking at me with a raised eyebrow.

"Oh my God!" Blair said pushing past me and throwing herself at Jamie. She wrapped her arms tightly around his neck. "You're alive. We knocked on your door. I thought you were dead!"

Jamie glanced in my direction as he hugged her back. He slowly tried to ease himself back, but she leaned forward and kissed him on the lips.

He placed his hands on her shoulders and stepped back, his eyes darting around the room nervously. "Yeah," he said with a chuckle, "I'm alive, although I was a little nervous that wouldn't be the case."

"You got sick too?" Bronx said stepping forward as he stretched out his hand. "Bronx, and you are?"

"Jamie," he said taking his hand. The men exchanged a brisk shake, and when they released, Jamie was able to step around the counter and back into the living room. It seemed as though he wanted to put space between himself and Blair. If she noticed she didn't care, considering she was still smiling at him.

"What's your name?" Bronx asked looking me over.

I swallowed, wishing I was better at hiding my nerves. "Gwen."

"You were sick, weren't you?" Bronx hadn't taken his eyes off of me.

I nodded.

He turned toward Jamie. "How about you?"

"Earlier. Seems to have passed," Jamie said. "How about you all?"

Bronx and Maggie nodded.

"It was terrible, Jamie!" Blair said twisting her finger into her hair. "I thought I was going to die."

"Yeah," Jamie said, scratching the side of his head. "It was bad."

"So," I said crossing my arms. "Do any of you know what's going on out there?"

Bronx shook his head. "Some kind of attack. Stay indoors." He hesitated. "Do either of you know anything beyond that?"

Jamie and I both shook our heads at the same time. I glanced at Blair who was staring at the bottle of water on my counter. She smiled at me when she caught me watching her.

"How do you know Jamie?" she asked, and my clothes suddenly felt scratchy.

"Just from the hall," I said.

"Okay," she said keeping the smile pasted to her face. Blair turned to Jamie. "You were here when this all happened?"

Jamie looked as though he was chewing his cheek. "No," Jamie said shifting his weight back and forth. "I came here after the attack or whatever it is that's going on."

"I see," Blair said.

"Well, we're going to keep looking for others, if you guys want to join us," Bronx said his eyes slightly narrowed.

I shook my head. "I'm just going to wait here."

"Me too," Jamie added swiftly.

Bronx nodded as he looked back and forth between Jamie and me. "You mind if we stop back later? You know, to touch base."

"Um," I stammered. I bit my lip nearly too hard as I shook my head. It just felt weird having strangers in my apartment, but I didn't know how to explain without offending anyone.

"We understand," Bronx said stretching his hand out once again toward Jamie. "I didn't mean to intrude or anything like that, but with the shit that's going down, we should probably stick together."

Maggie's eyes were red as she nodded. "I watched my boyfriend die."

She seemed to be in some kind of state of shock.

"I'm sorry," I said.

Bronx placed his hand on her shoulder. "We'll get out of your hair. Hopefully, we'll find others who managed to survive whatever the fuck this is. Maybe some answers." He turned to me and grinned. "Excuse my French."

"Right of course," I said following them as they walked toward the door. Bronx gave me one final look before stepping out into the hallway. "Thanks for stopping by."

He chuckled and dipped his head before leaving my apartment. The second I closed the door and locked it, I sucked in a long breath.

"Are you okay?" Jamie asked.

"I'm not good at this. I need to sit down."

"Good at what?"

I lowered myself down softly onto my sofa and pressed my palms against the sides of my face. My breaths quickened, and I could feel my anxiety rising.

"Any of this. I hate not knowing, yet I'm terrified to know."

"Yeah," Jamie said sitting down on the chair. He stared at his fingers as he twisted them against one another.

Everyone out there was in a different situation than I was. Like Maggie, for example, she'd watched her boyfriend die, whereas I didn't have anyone. I didn't have anyone to worry about, or anywhere to go.

My brother may have been out there, and my grandma, but she lived miles away. Hopefully, she was safe from whatever had happened.

But when I thought of my grandma... I started to worry. Maybe this wasn't just something happening locally. What if it were widespread? She could be out there scared. Suffering.

The urge to go to her was overwhelming. My pulse quickened, and I stood up. I could feel Jamie's eyes on me as I walked from room to room.

At some point, I'd have to find a way to go to her. If I could make it to my car, maybe I could get to her.

My grandma might need me. She'd been there for me all my life. I was all she had left. It wasn't like she could count on Nick. No one could.

For now, the sky was still too red. If I went out there, it could kill me, assuming that whatever was out there was what had made me sick. It had to have been. What else could have done it?

Maybe Jamie would come with me. I couldn't even tell him about it yet. He'd think I'd lost my mind.

"Want something to eat?" I asked as I stopped abruptly in front of him. I wasn't the least bit hungry, well, maybe I was, but I didn't feel hungry.

"Not really," Jamie said, gently patting his stomach. "Not sure I could keep much down."

"You kept the bar down," I reminded him.

Jamie nodded. "And that's about all I need at this point. If you're hungry, go for it. Don't let me stop you."

"No, I'm fine. I just wanted to be a good hostess."

Jamie chuckled. "I can't imagine having a better hostess in the middle of a disaster."

"Thanks, I think."

I sat down on the sofa, pulling my knees up to my chest. Even though I could see the redness coming through the window, it felt as though I was trapped inside of a dream. How could this be real? Why wasn't I freaking out, screaming and shouting for help?

Maybe because there wasn't anyone left to hear me.

The rest of the day ticked by slowly. Jamie and I took turns pacing. At one point I tried to read a book, but after I read the same sentence ten times, I gave up.

"Do you have any candles?" Jamie asked as the sun started to go down and the redness lighting the apartment started to turn to black.

"Yeah, I think so." I pushed myself off of the sofa and opened the drawer in the kitchen filled with junk. I pulled out two long taper candles and two small glass holders.

I set one down on the kitchen table and the other on the coffee table in the living room. The yellow glow from the candles mixed with the slight reddish hue still coming from outside gave my apartment an odd orange glow.

"Let me get you a pillow and a blanket," I said walking past Jamie and disappearing into my bedroom.

The flimsy faux wood closet door squeaked as I opened it. I stood on my tiptoes and pulled down an old pillow and a blanket I wished I would have washed recently.

I hugged them close to my chest as I turned to my bed remembering how sick I'd been. My sheets had been soaked when sweat had been pouring out of me and the trash bin... oh God, the trash bin.

I walked into the living room and placed the blanket on the sofa. Jamie hadn't turned away from the window.

"Sorry, I don't have anything nicer," I said.

"It's perfect. Thanks." Jamie sighed. "Shit. I should probably leave and just go back to my place."

"No," I said quickly. "I mean, if you want to obviously I can't stop you, but I like having the company. Having you here might just be keeping me from entirely losing my shit."

Jamie nodded. His mood had seemed to change ever since he'd seen Blair. I wasn't about to question it. Maybe it had nothing to do with her, whoever she was.

"Well, I'm going to go tidy up. Please make yourself at home."

"Thanks," he said finally turning from the window to offer me a small smile.

"Yeah, no problem," I said giving him an identical one back.

I checked the lock on the door and grabbed my bottle of water before heading back to my room. It wasn't long before I heard the sofa squeak from Jamie's weight.

That's what it was. He was tired. I couldn't blame him.

FIVE

After I finished cleaning up and changing my sheets, I took one last look out of the window hoping that things would look like normal again. But they didn't.

There were no streetlights, in fact, there was no light at all. If the moon was out, either clouds or whatever created the red sky was blocking it from giving off any light. Everything outside the window was pitch black.

And quiet.

If it hadn't been for the candles, I wasn't sure I'd be able to see my way around my apartment at all. At least with Jamie in the other room, I was a tiny bit less afraid than I would be if I'd been alone.

There weren't any sounds outside the window. No sounds of the city running as usual. There were no cars, no horns, no soft hum of electricity. The silence chilled my still slightly feverish bones.

As I stared out into the darkness, I had an eerie feeling that someone was standing behind me. I quickly turned expecting to see Jamie standing there, but there wasn't anyone there.

My finger trembled as I brought it up to my lip to gnaw on my fingernail. A nervous habit that I'd had since I was five.

As I was about to step away from the window, something caught my eye. There was a light.

The light from three flashlights bounced up and down as whoever was carrying them traversed the yard. It was a small group of people, but from where I stood, I couldn't tell anything about them.

I couldn't see if they were sick. And I couldn't tell if they were here to help us. For all I knew, it was Bronx, Blair, and Maggie looking for survivors.

They kept moving across the yard, moving slowly from left to right. My eyes moved along with them, following their lights as they moved across the ground.

When the group stopped, my breath felt like it

was stuck in my throat. They flashed the lights at one another briefly before pointing them around in various directions as if they were discussing which way to go.

I swallowed hard, and the action pinched my throat. The gulping noise I'd made sounded much too loud in the silence, and I wondered if Jamie had heard it in the other room.

My feet were glued in place as I watched them. Perhaps Bronx, Blair, and Maggie decided to leave the apartment and go find help, but it was far too dark to see who it was.

One of the lights moved across the yard toward the apartment building. My body stiffened, and my lungs forced the breath I'd been holding out. The breath I instantly sucked in was sharp in painful in the center of my chest.

I could see the light as it moved up the exterior wall, moving closer and closer toward my window. Just as it hit the glass, I took an abrupt step back. It was like something pulled me away.

Had they seen me? Why didn't I want to be seen?

I was too afraid to step closer and see if they were still out there. The light was gone from the window, but I still couldn't move.

I wasn't sure why I was so frightened, after all, whoever was out there might be there to help us. Maybe I wanted them to see me. Maybe I should have jumped up and down, pounded on the window, and waved my arms until they saw me.

But I hadn't.

And I wasn't sure why I hadn't. It was just a feeling deep in my gut that had made me leery.

For all I knew, I'd just let the only chance for Jamie and me to be rescued walk away. Then again, if whoever was out there had been here to help, they probably would have done more than flashed a light on the building in the middle of the night.

When someone knocked on the apartment door, it felt as though my heart had actually stopped for a moment. After a few seconds, it kicked back in and was pounding harder and faster against my chest.

I walked toward the living room, and the second I stepped out of my bedroom Jamie was standing in front of me. My hand went to my chest, and my knees buckled. I couldn't tell which part of my body was going to give out first... my legs or my heart.

"Shit, sorry," he said reaching out to hold me up. "I didn't mean to... it's just that... someone's at the door."

"I heard," I whispered.

"Are we going to open it?" Jamie asked.

I held onto his shoulder because I was afraid that if I let go, I'd crash to the floor. "Depends."

"On what?"

"Who it is."

SIX

The knocks were sharper. Urgent. And it felt like each knock was vibrating through my body and rattling my organs.

"It's us. Can we please come in?"

I recognized the voice. It was Bronx. The guy from earlier.

"Want me to send them away?" Jamie asked.

"It's fine." I stepped past him and walked toward the door. Before I opened it, I peeked out to make sure I was right about who was standing outside my door.

My fingers shook as I unlocked the door and stepped back slightly.

"They're all dead," Bronx said, his voice heavy. "Please, can we come in?"

I swallowed but stepped to the side. It wasn't like I could have sent them away. They all looked far more afraid than they had when I'd seen them earlier.

Once they were all inside, I closed the door. The room was dark, but I could see Blair's eyes as they locked onto the pillow and blanket on the sofa. Her lips curled upward slightly into a satisfied smile.

"Sorry, I know you didn't want us to come back," Bronx said crossing his arms as he stepped in front of me. "But it's just us. We're all that's left."

"Maybe others aren't answering their door," Jamie said.

Bronx nodded. "It's possible. But some doors were open. We could see, and it's similar to the scene outside of your door in the hallway."

"We all got sick," Maggie said. "For some reason, we survived."

"Immunity?" I asked so softly it seemed as though no one had heard me.

Bronx took a step closer. "Is there any chance I could talk to you... privately?"

"Um...." My eyes shifted toward Jamie for a second before turning back to Bronx. I jerked my chin toward my bedroom. "This way."

We stepped into my bedroom and Bronx reached

over my shoulder, closing the door nearly all the way behind us. He was so close I could smell his woodsy, masculine deodorant.

Bronx moved away from me slowly and stared down into my eyes. A small amount of light slithered through the small space between the door and the door frame striping his face.

"What can I do for you?" I said shifting my wait to put a bit more distance between us.

"I think we all need to stay together." Bronx held up his hand. "Before you say no, let me tell you why we all need to stick together."

I tilted my head to the side waiting for him to go on. It wasn't like I even had any more room in my apartment, and I definitely didn't have any more pillows.

"If we're all that's left, we can help each other. We can work together to find food and water. Who knows when we'll get the all clear."

My jaw was stiff, and I was sure Bronx noticed the tension even in the darkness. "I don't have enough room or blankets. And the food I have... well, I need it."

"We can get our own food from our own apartments or from one of the other now unoccupied rooms." Bronx's eyes shifted toward the cracked door. "We can find our own pillows and blankets... sleep on the floor. It's just that I think it's better if we all stay together. We won't be a bother. I promise."

"Well," I said watching as a shadow moved past the door. Someone was trying to listen in, and I was pretty sure it was Jamie. "It's okay with me I guess if it's okay with Jamie."

"Are you two like—"

"No!" I said too sharply. "I barely know him, but he was here first."

I tried not to roll my eyes at myself. It was hard to explain, but I felt close to Jamie. Probably because I'd known him a little before the attack.

"Blair said she used to date him," Bronx said, his voice feather soft.

"Oh," I said, putting the pieces together. The kiss she'd planted on him. Her noticing where he was sleeping. Maybe she wasn't entirely over him, which I could totally understand considering Jamie was extremely good-looking.

"You sound disappointed."

I cocked my head to the side. "I do not. And I am not. There was some kind of attack, and you think I'm worried about who Jamie dated?"

I wanted to stomp away from him, but it was my bedroom. It was odd that Jamie hadn't mentioned it, but then again, why would he? He had no obligations to explain anything about why Blair had thrown herself into his arms.

"Well, if it's all right with Jamie and you all don't mind sleeping on the floor, then I guess you're welcome to stay."

Bronx nodded and reached over my shoulder again, opening the door. I held myself stiff, refusing to look at him as he walked past me.

He boldly walked over to Jamie and began telling him all the same things he'd told me. After he finished, Jamie simply shrugged and said that if it was okay with me, then it was okay with him too.

"It's settled then," Bronx said clapping his hands and flashing me a cocky grin. "We're a team."

And it seemed as though Bronx had already promoted himself to team lead. Not that it really mattered to me considering what was happening outside wasn't giving us a lot of options anyway.

"All right," Bronx said rubbing his hands together. "The first thing we need to do is go back to our apartments and get some blankets and pillows."

"I don't want to go back to my apartment," Maggie said, tucking stray hairs behind her ear.

Blair placed her hand on Maggie's shoulder. "I'm sure we can find some stuff at my place."

"We'll be back," Bronx said walking over to the door. He hesitated, turned, and locked eyes with me. A grin grew on his face. "You'll let us back in, right?"

"Yes," I said pressing my lips together.

"Perfect. Be back in a few." Bronx, Blair, and Maggie stepped out into the hall, and walked across the room, locking the door after them.

I exhaled loudly as I slowly paced the floor. My eyes shifted over to the sofa where Jamie had been resting.

"I'm sorry about this," I said.

"What are you sorry for?" Jamie asked, his narrowed eyes barely visible in the darkness.

"This was your space, and now you have roommates."

Jamie chuckled. "This was your space... I'm the one that forced myself into your territory. Nothing is stopping me from going back to my apartment."

"Still," I said shaking my head. "You were here first."

"Don't give it another thought," Jamie said, the floor creaking as he walked over to the sofa. He groaned as he sat down, running his hands through his messy hair. "Do you think this is smart though? I mean, we don't know anything about them."

I cocked my head to the side. It wasn't like I'd

known much about Jamie either but that hadn't stopped us from teaming up.

"Seems to me you know Blair," I said unable to stop the words from seeping out between my lips.

Jamie's body tensed for a brief moment. "We dated. Still, we don't know anything about Maggie or Bronx."

"Have you ever seen them around here?" I asked.

"Yeah," Jamie said. "They all lived here. Even talked to Maggie's boyfriend a few times. He was a good guy."

All of this was making me realize just how much I had kept to myself. The only reason I knew Jamie at all was because he lived down the hall. Socializing made me anxious. Hell, people made me anxious. Now here I was, feeling as though I had no choice in the matter.

"I'm sure it'll be fine," Jamie said glancing at me over his shoulder.

"Are you?" I said raising my brows although he couldn't see me.

"Having them here will be fine. What happens out there is anyone's guess."

I nodded, but still, he couldn't see me. Even though it was night, the apartment started to feel warm. Little droplets of sweat gathered at my temples. Maybe it wasn't heat, maybe my fever was coming back.

I sighed and combed my fingers through my hair as I walked over to the window. My body was craving rest and after what I'd gone through, I knew I needed it. Even though there was going to be a group of strangers in my apartment, I hoped I'd be able to get some sleep. I also hoped my insomnia would stay away for the rest of the night.

There was only darkness as I peered out between the curtains. Whoever had been out there was long gone.

It wasn't long until the others returned. They'd brought blankets and plastic bags filled with food.

Maggie set up her sleeping area on the floor next to the TV and Blair set hers up near the sofa. Bronx spread out his blanket near the window and sat down resting his back against the wall.

Everyone was quiet, and no one seemed even a little bit comfortable, not that they complained. It wasn't like I was going to be all that comfortable in my bed and it was my place. Everything was a mess, and the only thing we could do was to make the best of it.

And try to survive whatever was happening.

SEVEN

I tossed and turned most of the night, but I'd slept better than some of the recent nights since losing my job. My body was doing what it could to get well, and in fact, when I woke, I was warm, but I felt okay. Hungry, but okay.

I sat up and listened, but there were no sounds coming from the other room. It wouldn't surprise me to be the first one up, after all, it was still dark outside, but I could tell it would be morning soon.

The electricity was still out, I could tell from the lack of humming, not to mention my alarm clock would have turned back on. I pressed the button on my phone even though I knew nothing would happen.

The room felt warm, perhaps from the lack of air

conditioning or maybe it was from whatever was going on outside.

I stepped over to the blinds, slowly moving them to peek out between them. Most everything was still dark, but there was a slight orangish glow rising above the horizon where the sun would soon come up. Without a doubt, I knew the sky would still be red.

I waited in my room, watching the sky change colors as the sun started to rise. It was probably at least an hour before I'd heard someone moving in my living room.

There was a big part of me that wanted to stay hidden in my bedroom until everything blew over, but there was another part of me that knew I couldn't. I'd have to go out there even though none of us knew anything more today than we did yesterday.

I wrapped my arms around my middle and stepped out of my bedroom. Jamie instantly turned and looked at me, Blair wide awake near his feet.

"Morning," Jamie said, pushing himself off of the sofa and walking over toward me.

"Morning," I said looking around the room. The others were all awake although none of them had moved from their sleeping areas.

Jamie followed me into the kitchen, and I offered

him a fresh bottle of water. We both unscrewed the caps at the same time and took a big swallow.

"It seems less," Bronx said jerking his thumb toward the window.

I nodded, but I wasn't sure if I agreed. Someone had blown out the candles, and the amount of light we'd had inside the apartment seemed about the same as yesterday.

"So, I was thinking," Bronx said pushing himself to his feet. He pushed his shoulders back and stepped into the kitchen area joining Jamie and me. Having him there made the already small kitchen feel smaller. "Maybe we should go around and gather supplies from the other apartments. Pack some in bags in case we need to leave."

"Like go through other people's things?" I asked.

"They won't be needing them," Bronx said with an uncaring shrug. "It's just that what if we're forced to leave? We'll want to make sure we'll have everything we need."

Jamie crossed his arms. "What would make us leave? We're supposed to stay indoors, at least that's the last I heard."

"And it seems that's the last any of us will hear," Bronx snorted.

"We don't know that," I said holding up a hand. I

could feel the tension in the room being pulled tighter, like a stretched rubber band.

"No, we don't know, but I think it's best if we're prepared," Bronx clasped his hands loosely in front of him. "What if there's a fire?"

Blair took several steps closer. "I think it's a great idea, Bronx. If I can do anything to help, just let me know."

"Of course you can help. I think we should all go together," Bronx said. "We'll each fill two bags... watching each other's backs."

I looked at Jamie, and he offered me a barely there shrug. No matter how hard I tried, I couldn't come up with an excuse not to go along.

"Okay," I said. Perhaps Bronx was right. Maybe his plan was smart... it wasn't like I had any idea what to do. He was being proactive. Wanting to position ourselves better in an already shitty situation.

And we had nothing else to do with our days. Sitting in the red apartment staring at the walls probably wasn't good for any of us. Getting out and keeping ourselves busy, hoping that we were doing something that might help us was probably the right choice.

"Awesome," Bronx said rubbing his hands together excitedly.

He started going into detail about the types of bags we'd look for as well as all the things we'd put inside.

"How do you know so much about all of this stuff?" Blair asked.

"I don't know anything." Bronx shrugged. "Other than having done some reading on the subject."

"Which subject?" Jamie asked.

Bronx blinked, keeping his eyes wide. "Survival."

My stomach swirled. Not from illness but from the very mention of the word. Survival. Was that what this was?

Deep down I think I knew it was, but it wasn't something I was able to wrap my head around. How could this be real? What if no one came for us? What if there wasn't anything left?

My heart started to race, and the beads of sweat at my temples increased. I willed myself not to have a panic attack in front of everyone. That was the last thing any of us needed... me freaking out.

Bronx stared at me as if he could hear the blood pumping through my veins. He placed his hand on my shoulder and gave a light squeeze.

"We got this," he whispered as he stepped around me and into the living room. "Gwen?"

"Yeah?" I said sucking in an awkward, sharp breath.

"Got any bags?"

I dug through my closet and found an old bag I used when I'd traveled to my grandma's. It was in good condition because I hadn't used it all that much.

We were each going to go through our own apartments and pack anything that was important. Then if we still needed more, we'd go through the now vacant rooms.

The others gave me space as I filled my bag. I put in an old flashlight, a change of clothes, some bandages, and other things I thought might come in handy, like snacks.

When I was finished, I left my bag hidden in my closet, locked my apartment door, and followed the group to Jamie's room. He quickly filled two bags that had his delivery company's logo on it while we waited in his living room.

His apartment was a level of clean I'm not sure I'd ever witnessed before. The only thing that had been out of place was the blanket that was draped over the back of his sofa.

Jamie worked quickly. His eyes darted over to us every so often. If he was worried about us looking through his things, he had nothing to worry about considering he barely had any things.

After we finished at Jamie's, we went to Bronx's, and then to Maggie's. She stood there staring at the numbers on her door, her shoulders rising and falling with each breath.

"I can't do it," she said.

"No problem," Blair said with a smile. "We'll find stuff for you at my place."

At Blair's, Jamie, Bronx, and I sat on the sofa waiting as she thoroughly went through every room, drawer, and cabinet. I wanted to remind her that we'd just be upstairs and if she remembered anything we could always come down for it, but I kept my mouth shut. It wasn't like I was really in a hurry to get back to my apartment and wait for what I wasn't even sure.

"Okay!" she said with a bag over one shoulder and a purse over the other. I glanced at Jamie and tried to picture the two of them as a couple. I couldn't see it. "Ready?"

Bronx smacked his palms against his thighs and pushed himself up. "Let's go."

I followed the others out of the apartment, Jamie directly behind me. Blair stopped and locked her apartment door, she smiled when she saw me watching her. She dangled her keys in front of me and tucked them into her pocket as she pushed her way between Jamie and me.

At the end of the hall where the main entrance was, Bronx had stopped. His eyes focused on something I couldn't see.

"What is it?" Jamie asked.

"The door's been broken," Bronx said gesturing for us to follow him up the stairs. "It wasn't like that yesterday."

As we walked by, I looked into the entrance way at what remained of the glass door. Bits of glass were sprinkled all over the floor, and I wasn't sure, but it looked like there was a small pool of blood just outside the door frame.

"What happened?" I asked keeping my voice soft.

"No idea," Jamie said with a hard swallow. "But I don't like it."

"Me either."

The stairs sounded exceptionally noisy as we made our way up to the second floor. I couldn't shake the feeling that someone was behind us even though I glanced over my shoulder every few seconds to check.

When we got back up to the room, I unlocked

the door. Standing back as I allowed the others to enter first. Bronx and Jamie both stood there behind me.

Jamie gestured at the door.

"Go ahead," Bronx said nearly at the same time as he flashed me with a smile. "Jamie you want to help me move a few bodies? If we don't do it soon, the smell is going to kill us."

"Um, sure," Jamie said.

Before I could even take a step, there were noises in the stairwell. Someone was coming.

EIGHT

"Get inside!" Bronx said nearly picking me up off of the ground when I didn't move fast enough.

I wanted to ask what he was nervous about. For all we knew, it was someone coming to help us.

"Why are you scared?" I hissed.

"I just want to be sure," he said, the words spilling out of his mouth as he wrapped his arms around me and lifted me off of the ground.

"Hey!" the voice from the stairwell called out. He aimed a gun in our direction as he took small steps forward. "Put her down."

I blinked several times trying to make sense of what I was seeing in the darkness. "Nick?"

Bronx narrowed his eyes at me. He didn't let go, but he loosened his grip.

"Yeah, who are these guys?" Nick said his voice deep and authoritative.

"Friends," I said wiggling myself free. "Could you stop aiming that thing at us?"

"I'm not aiming it at you," Nick said, his eyes fixed on Bronx. He hesitated, but reluctantly lowered the gun, tucking it into the holster on his hip.

Bronx tilted his head to the side and pushed his shoulders back. "You know this guy?"

"I do... he's my brother," I said pressing my lips together.

"How did you get here?" Bronx asked.

"I'll be glad to tell you all about it inside my sister's apartment," Nick said, looking anxiously over his shoulder. He held out his arms attempting to usher us inside.

Blair and Maggie stood close to one another as they eyed Nick. Maggie looked at him suspiciously, but Blair's expression turned into something that made me roll my eyes. The little curl to her lips and the batting eyelashes were sickening.

I locked the door before introducing everyone to

my brother. Nick looked at the backpacks and nodded approvingly.

"Looks like you're in good hands," Nick said.

"Do you know what's going on out there?" I asked.

Nick shook his head. "I had my scanner going, but they weren't talking about it until it happened. Something in the air, a chemical of some kind. They sent out every officer, but they didn't report back. Then everything went out. EMP or something I'm guessing."

"Some kind of poisonous attack and an EMP?" Bronx asked skeptically.

"It seems that way, but I don't know for sure. I'm not sure we'll ever know." Nick shook his head. "Depends on who's still out there, and I can tell you, it's not good."

My stomach twisted like someone was wringing it like it was a towel. I twisted my shaking fingers together hoping no one noticed how much I was shaking.

"How widespread is this?" I asked.

Nick sighed. "I don't know."

"What does it look like out there? You didn't get sick?" Bronx asked. He looked as though he was full of questions.

"It's not pretty," Nick said scratching the side of his neck. "Bodies all over. Lots of people got sick. Lots of people died."

"And you?" Bronx asked again. "Did you get sick?"

Nick studied me for a moment before nodding his head. "I did, but it's gone. I'm fine. I'm not contagious."

"Well, you don't know that," I said before letting out a sigh. I pressed my fingertips to my temple. "We all were sick and got better. I can't believe you're here."

I gawked at him. It was strange having him inside of my apartment. I didn't know what to do, say, or think. What he'd done to our family was still in my head, but it was nice to see a familiar face amid the chaos and confusion.

"Can I have something to drink?" Nick asked pressing his hand to his throat. "I haven't had anything in a while."

"Um, sure," I said stepping around him and into my kitchen. I took one of the bottles out of the warm fridge. "Here."

"Thanks," Nick said staring into my eyes. He lowered his voice. "Can we talk? Somewhere else?"

I swallowed hard as my eyes darted around the

room. It was one thing having him here with the others around but being alone with him was another story. I didn't want to get into a conversation that was going to upset me. Or make me want to send him away. And it made me mad that I didn't want to send him away.

"I'm not sure that's a good idea," I said.

"Please?"

"Fine. Make it quick." I flicked my wrist toward my bedroom. "We'll just be a minute," I announced.

Jamie and I locked eyes briefly as I led Nick to my room. I forced a smile in his direction, but Jamie didn't give me one back.

After I closed the door, Nick stepped forward and gave me a hug. It was stiff and awkward, but he didn't seem to notice. He stepped back, and something that resembled fear filled his eyes.

"I was so worried about you," Nick.

"Why?" I asked shaking my head.

"Because you're my sister."

I couldn't stop my eyes from rolling. "I guess there is a first time for everything."

It was a low blow, and it wasn't exactly true. When we were younger, we were the best of friends. Unfortunately, as adults, things had changed.

"Gwen, please. What happened... it's done.

Things have changed with me. It's time for us to move on."

I almost choked as I blew out a heavy puff of air. "I'll never be able to move on."

"We're all we have left."

"That's not true. We have grandma," I said forcing my voice to hold steady.

"Maybe." Nick shrugged. "I mean I hope so, but the world out there has changed. I know you haven't seen it, but I have. Nothing will ever be the same. We have to stay together."

I sighed and shook my head.

"Gwen, seriously, I loved her too. She wasn't just your mom, she was mine too."

"Then you should have acted that way when she was alive. You should have gone to her. You should have told her how you felt before she died," I spat.

Nick walked over to the window and peeked out of the blinds. He lowered his head.

"I went to see her before it... I told her exactly how I felt. And how sorry I was. She knew. You can be angry, hate me, blame me, whatever. No one will ever be harder on me about what happened that I am."

He ran his hands through his hair. His eyes

shifted up for a moment connecting with mine so quickly I wasn't even sure it had happened.

"It was better if I stayed away from you. You were all better off without me. After I lost my job on the force... none of you needed to see me like that."

"That's just ridiculous. She would still be alive if you would have just—"

"Gwen, she committed suicide. It wasn't because I couldn't stop using. She was sick." My bed squeaked as he sat down heavily on the mattress. "She told me she wasn't in there because of me. She said it wasn't my fault. Of course, I don't believe that, but it's what she said. She told me she'd be fine."

I hadn't realized it, but tears were streaming down my cheeks.

"But I shouldn't have left her that day. If I would have stayed at her side, she wouldn't have been able to go through with it." Nick lowered his head into his hands. His fingertips were tight against his scalp as his fingers tightened and pulled his hair at the roots. "They told me she would have just picked another day. She was depressed. The medicine wasn't work-ing... maybe it was making it worse."

"Who told you that?"

"The nurses at the institution. I went back there and talked to them. Well, first I went there to yell, I made a pretty big scene, but they calmed me." Nick glanced upward. "They didn't want me to blame myself."

I shook my head. "She couldn't stand what you were doing to yourself. To the family. We all wanted to help you, but you wouldn't listen."

"I know that, Gwen. I know that. But I didn't want help." Nick stood abruptly holding out his arms. "I'm clean now. Been clean. I've been trying to find a way to come to talk to you, but I just hadn't figured out how, or when."

"You're only clean because you have no way of getting your fix with what's going on out there."

"Probably easier to get a fix now than it was before. And far cheaper." Nick shook his head. "I've been clean for six months."

"Ooh six months," I said hating my tone. I should have been more supportive, but I still blamed him. And maybe I always would.

"Look, if you want me to leave, I'll go. I want to stay with you, but if you don't want me here, I understand." Nick stepped past me and put his hand on the doorknob. I could hear feet shuffling away on the other side of the door.

"You don't have to go," I said, pressing my palm against the back of my head. He was my brother. Yes,

I was still angry, but I couldn't send him out there if everything were really as bad as he was making it seem. "I want to go to grandma. I need to make sure she's okay."

Nick nodded. "Of course. I'll go with you." He pointed at the gun on his hip. "I'll protect you."

"How likely is it we'll need that?" I asked.

"We will definitely need it." Nick shifted his weight from one foot to the other. "When do we leave?"

I let out a long sigh as I turned to face the door. For all I knew, the others all had someone they wanted to look for too.

I wasn't sure what to do, or how to tell the others. Before I decided, I needed to know more about what Nick had seen. "I'm not sure yet. Soon."

NINE

W e were all sitting in the living room, except for Nick who was standing in front of us with his hands behind his back. Jamie was next to me on the sofa, his hands tightly clasped in his lap.

"There was so much devastation out there," Nick said, shifting his gaze toward the window. "At times, I wasn't even sure if I'd make it here alive."

Maggie hugged her knees to her chest and stared up at him. I hated the way both Blair and Maggie looked at him. They didn't know what kind of man he was. They didn't know he'd rather get high than come to his mom's fiftieth birthday party.

Of course, it was probably better they didn't. Nick had told the others he used to be a cop, but what he didn't tell them was that he got kicked off for doing drugs before, during, and after work. Drugs that he took from the station.

He also didn't tell them that he told our mom to go to fucking hell when she was crying and pleading for him to get help. Not long before she died.

"There are so many bodies out there. The smell is something I can't even describe. Rotting, diseased flesh," Nick said swallowing hard. "But that's not all."

Nick started to pace but then stopped abruptly. He turned to us again.

"I saw a man shoot another for his wallet and a pack of fruit snacks." Nick shook his head. "His wallet. Like with everything that's going on out there, he was worried about money."

"That's so scary," Blair said softly.

Nick nodded. "I could hear people crying... screaming out for help. But as far as I could tell, there is no help. No police. No military. No one is out there. Not even an ambitious security guard."

"There must be someone somewhere. Maybe they just haven't made it this far yet," Blair said.

"Maybe," Nick said. "But until they do, we're all on our own."

"We'll just stay here until help comes," Maggie said with a half-shrug.

Nick looked at me. He knew I wanted to go out there to make our way to our grandma's farm. But I wasn't about to mention it. At least not yet.

"Help might not come," Bronx said staring at Nick. "We won't be able to stay here forever."

"But we can stay for a long time," Maggie said. "There's enough food here to last us weeks."

"We can stay for now," Nick said with a single bob of his head. "We'll have to come up with a plan."

Maggie sniffed hard. "What kind of plan?"

"A way to get ourselves safe again," Nick said.

"We're not safe here?" Maggie asked in a voice that was almost nonexistent.

Nick knelt down in front of her and took her hand into his. "I honestly don't know. It's better in here than it is out there. We'll figure this out. We'll find a way to get help."

I watched Nick as he tried to comfort Maggie. He almost seemed as though he actually cared. His voice was fluffy and comforting, and it seemed to be working on Maggie.

Nick patted the back of her hand and stood up again. "But even though I think we're okay inside of Gwen's apartment for now, doesn't mean it will stay that way. I don't want to get anyone a false sense of security. We need to be safe, smart... vigilant."

Bronx nodded along. At first he'd seemed skeptical of Nick, but the more he listened to my brother talk the more he seemed to like him.

Nick continued talking about the town. How everything looked the same but soaked in red. There were no friendly faces. Death was everywhere.

Blair had asked how many people he'd seen in all, but it had only been a handful in a city of a couple million. That was a shock to all of us.

Nick talked for hours, occasionally interrupted by a question from one of the others. He wouldn't ever admit it, but I could tell he was enjoying every second. I wondered if it reminded him of when he'd been a police officer.

It was probably around dinner time when I stood up and walked to the kitchen. The only two people that seemed to notice was Jamie and Nick. Nick kept talking and enjoyed being the center of attention, but Jamie followed me.

"You okay?" he asked softly as I took out a box of cereal and started munching on it.

"Yeah," I said forcing a smile that wrinkled my brow, as I tipped the box in Jamie's direction.

He took a handful and poured a few pieces into his mouth. "Are you sure about that?"

"No, yeah, I am. It's just I'm still tired. You know,

probably from what our bodies had gone through," I said unable to stop my eyes from moving away from Jamie's intense blue eyes and setting them on his chest.

"Yeah, I understand. I still kind of feel like I'm recovering from being hit by a truck."

I nodded and shoveled more cereal into my mouth. It wasn't like I could tell Jamie but having everyone around was getting to me. My skin was starting to crawl having everyone around twenty-four-seven. It just wasn't something I was used to.

I was about to excuse myself to my bedroom when there was a noise at the window. My eyes locked with Jamie's and Nick stopped talking.

"Did you hear that?" I asked.

Jamie nodded. His lips pressed tightly together as if he didn't want to make a sound.

Nick held up his palm, and my apartment was once again that eerie, absolute silence I'd only ever heard during a thunderstorm when all the power went out.

After about a minute it happened again. A sharp ping against the window.

"Hey," a voice called out. It was faint, but I could tell by the looks on the other's faces that they'd heard it too.

I took small steps as I walked over to the window. It looked like Nick wanted me to stop, to ignore it, but I couldn't.

When I got to the window, a hand grabbed mine, just as I reached out to the curtain. Nick was standing next to me, slowly shaking his head from side to side.

My eyes filled with a red anger that matched the outside sky and Nick reluctantly let go of my hand.

We both jumped when something pinged against the window again.

"God dammit," Nick whispered.

I eased my body closer, keeping it pressed tightly to the wall. My breathing steady as I looked out of the small space between the window and the curtain.

There was a man out there, staring up at the window. He knelt down and picked up a small stone.

"Someone's out there," I said quietly without turning away. "He's throwing rocks at the windows."

"Why?" Blair asked quietly.

I ignored her question, not because I wanted to, but because I didn't have the answer.

Nick carefully inched over to the other side and peeked out. "Jesus."

It was just the one man, and for some reason, he

was mostly concentrating his efforts on my window. He threw another pebble.

"Please! Someone! Help me!" he shouted.

The man didn't appear to be well. Somehow, he was standing out there, but even from the second floor, I could see the sores on his face. Most of his hair had fallen out, but there were patches of it left in various spots on his head. It was like he'd managed to fight off the illness but not after it had damaged him.

"I see the light," the man shouted. "I know you're in there. Please!"

"We can't let him in," Nick said.

I could see the man's lips moving, but I couldn't hear what he was saying. He ran his hands through what was left of his hair, and when he pulled his hand away, there were clumps stuck between his fingers. The man looked horrified and shook his hand as if it were covered in bugs.

"The door downstairs is broken," Bronx said. "He could just walk in, come up to the room."

Nick's hand hovered over his gun.

"Nick," I said. "He's just trying to survive like we all are."

"We can't help him. What if he's still sick? He

could get us all sick again. We don't know him, and we can't trust him," Nick said.

"There has to be something we can do to help," I said chewing my cheek as I looked back out at the suffering man.

Several men stepped out from behind a building and started approaching the man. Each one of them carried a large gun and wore gas masks that hid their faces.

"Shit," Nick said. "Blow out the candle."

Maggie dashed across the living room and blew out the candle that was giving off a small glow on the kitchen table. My eyes were glued to the people on the ground below.

It appeared as though they were talking to the man. They kept their distance, but occasionally they would nod. After several minutes, the man pointed up toward my window

Nick and I both sharply moved back at nearly the same time. I sighed and shook my head.

"They can't see us," I whispered.

"You sure about that?" Nick asked cocking his head to the side.

I blew out a breath. "Sure enough."

I leaned forward and watched as the group of men led the sick man away.

"They're leaving," I said swallowing hard, watching as they disappeared from view.

I stepped to the side and pressed my palms against the wall. I sucked in a long breath as if I'd been rescued from drowning.

My eyes shifted over to Nick's. His shoulders were tensed up toward his ears. Just as his arms started to relax, the pop of a gun ripped through the air.

"Oh my God!" Maggie said.

"Jesus Christ," Nick said inside of his inhale.

"What did they do? What did they do to him?" Maggie asked, desperate for answers I didn't have. Her whole body was shaking, and she looked as though she might scream.

Bronx grabbed her shoulders and held her tightly as he looked into her eyes. "Stay calm. It's okay."

"They all want us dead. They've come to finish us off!" Maggie said, her wide eyes glowing in the increasing darkness.

"We're going to be okay," Bronx said, his thumbs moving up and down on her shoulders.

"No, we aren't," Maggie said letting her shoulders drop as if someone had placed ten-pound weights on them. "We're all going to die."

Bronx looked over his shoulder, first at me and

then at Nick. He whispered to Maggie as he led her into my bathroom.

I crossed my arms, refusing to look at the others. There wasn't anything stopping the men from coming into the apartment building. The main entrance door had been shattered. All they had to do was walk in and force their way through my apartment door.

Maybe getting to my grandma was going to be more of a challenge than I thought. If Nick's horror stories were true, it would be difficult making our way out of town, and that wasn't even considering food or if the illness would still find a way to take us.

I caught Nick's eye, and it almost seemed as though he could tell what was on my mind. His eyes were softer, but he didn't even try to say anything that might ease my worries.

But seeing and hearing the close gunshot, only made me want to go see my grandma more. She needed me.

TEN

When I got up the next morning, Nick was sitting near the window with his back against the wall. His knees were up, and his gun dangled out of his hand between them.

"Did you sleep?" I asked looking out of the window. The sky was still red, but I was almost sure it had lessened. Instead of being tomato red, it was blood orange.

"Not much. Was worried," Nick said nodding at the door.

My head bobbed. "We could have taken turns."

"It's fine. I'm not sure I could have slept anyway."

The others started to stir, and I glanced over at

Jamie. He'd been watching Nick and me, but quickly looked away when our eyes connected.

I turned to go to the kitchen, but Nick grabbed my arm. His eyes locked on to the pile of backpacks near the back closet.

"I think we need to come up with a plan to get out of here." Nick lowered his voice. "They could come back."

"Maybe that man was sick," I said, my voice equally quiet. "Maybe they had a reason."

"Maybe, but maybe not. There are people out there right now who would kill for those," Nick said his eyes still on the backpacks.

I pressed my lips together. "You're overreacting."

"I don't think I am. None of us are sick, I think we can go out there," Nick said.

I shook my head. "Those men had gas masks. Clearly, they don't think the air is safe."

"It'll be safer in the country," Nick said, turning his eyes to meet mine. "Less crazy people to worry about."

"How hard will it be to get out of town?" Bronx asked. He'd apparently been listening as well.

"I think we can manage," Nick said. "But we'll need to be careful."

Maggie popped up. "I'm not going out there."

"My grandma lives in the country. Her place is big enough for all of us, and I want to make sure she's okay," I said almost wishing I could take back my words. It wasn't like my grandma was going to like having guests any more than I did.

"We're safe here. We should stay here and wait for help," Maggie said, her eyebrows squeezing tightly together.

Nick shook his head. "We don't know if help is coming. If they do, it could take weeks, months, maybe even years. It's every man for himself."

"You don't know that," Jamie said, sitting up. His eyes were on his hands in his lap.

Nick stood. "You're right I don't know. All I can do is guess, and if Gwen wants to go to our grandma, I'm going with her. None of you need to come with us if you don't want to."

"I don't know when I'm going to go," I said grabbing my elbow.

"I'm worried about those men coming here," Nick said.

My hands dropped down to my sides. "I'm worried too, but I'm worried about rushing out there too."

"At some point, we're going to have to figure out

a plan," Nick said, and it seemed as though he was talking to me specifically.

"And we will," I said, ignoring Bronx as he looked over his shoulder at us. If there was something on his mind, he kept his mouth closed. "I need to eat. Excuse me."

I walked into the kitchen and grabbed whatever I could find from my cupboards. My eyes were down as I walked by everyone and shut myself in my bedroom.

There were so many thoughts racing through my head I couldn't eat. My stomach twisted and turned craving some food, but my mind wasn't allowing it.

I could hear them moving around outside my door, but I couldn't make out any of their soft whispers. It was probably better that I didn't because either way, I was going to attempt to make my way to my grandma.

There was a soft knock at the door. My head fell back as I worked to suppress a groan. I didn't feel like talking to Nick.

"Yes?" I said unable to keep the annoyed tone from my voice.

"Sorry, can I talk to you?" Jamie asked peeking his head into my room.

"Oh," I said letting out a breath. "Yeah, of course, come on in."

Jamie stepped inside closing the door behind him. He turned and blinked before looking around my room.

"You can sit if you'd like," I said tilting my head to the side.

"I could, but you'll probably kick me out after I say what I'm about to say," Jamie said, his jaw stiff.

"I doubt it." I flashed him a tight-lipped smile.

Jamie nodded and sat down, the bed squeaking with his weight. He stared at his hands as he slowly opened his mouth.

"I don't think we should go out there," he said.

"Get out of my room," I said, and Jamie turned to me. "Totally kidding."

Jamie chuckled, but his eyes were narrowed. He let out a breath and turned to me, his captivating ocean blue eyes staring into mine.

"It's just that I think we have it pretty good here as far as supplies are concerned." Jamie scratched the back of his neck.

"We packed the bags. I think we can make it, and my grandma has tons of food in storage. She loved to can stuff." I bit my lip and stared at the window. "If we can get there, I really think we'll all be safer."

"It's the if we get there part that makes me worried," Jamie said. "I don't want anything to happen to you... any of us."

It wasn't like I wanted anything to happen to anyone either, including myself. But I couldn't stop picturing my grandma sitting there at the window staring out, worried and scared about what was happening.

Her nearest neighbor was at least two miles away, and he had a family. It was highly unlikely that he was running out to her house to check on her.

"I noticed you didn't mention how far away she lives," Jamie said.

"It'll be a hike," I said twisting my fingers together. "But doable."

"You're still not saying," Jamie smiled.

I let out a short breath. "Don't freak out."

"Oh, that far, huh?"

"Less than two hundred miles."

"How much less?"

I blinked twice before forcing myself to look into his eyes. "She's roughly seventy-five miles from here."

"Are you kidding?" Jamie said standing up. He drew in a deep breath and lowered himself back down. "You're planning to walk seventy-five miles?"

"Yeah, it'll take a few days, but it's doable."

Jamie was shaking his head. "It's going to take more than a few days. If you walk five miles a day, it'll take you like fifteen days to get there."

"I think we can do more than five miles a day." I shrugged.

"I think you're giving everyone too much credit.

"We'll be motivated."

Jamie rubbed his palms roughly on his thighs. "Can I do anything to talk you out of this?"

"I don't think so," I said refusing to meet his gaze.

"What if she's... sick," Jamie said clearing his throat at the end of his sentence.

It felt like hands grabbed my heart and squeezed. "I'd want to know."

"Okay," Jamie said sliding his palms up and down his thighs. "Okay."

"I'm sorry," I said.

"Sorry for what?"

I looked into his eyes. "I have to do this."

"Yeah, I understand." Jamie's shoulders dropped as he let out a breath. "And I'll help you get there. If that's what you want."

"Yes," I said smiling. I hesitated before I wrapped my arms around his neck, hugging him. My arms quickly dropped, and I inched away. "I'd like that. It kind of feels like we're in this together."

"I know what you mean," Jamie said, flopping back on my bed. He reached over and lightly touched his fingers to my back. "I feel the same."

Our eyes met in the darkness, and even though I wanted to look away from the intensity of his gaze, I didn't. There was something in his eyes that held me tightly. I didn't want to look away.

"Argh," Jamie said as he crunched himself back into a seated position. "I guess I should get back out there."

"What's the rush?" I asked offering him my box of cereal.

Jamie grabbed the box and pulled out a handful. "Your brother is out there trying to rally the troops. Everyone is on board except for—"

"Maggie."

"Right. And we can't leave her here alone." I stood up and walked over to the window, peering out between the blinds. "And I don't think we're ready."

Jamie swallowed. "Nick's ready."

"Nick's not in charge."

"You might need to tell him that," Jamie said.

Every muscle in my body tensed. "I don't think he'll leave without me, but if he does, that's his choice." I turned, my hands clenched into tight fists at my side. "I'll go when I'm ready."

"Can I join in or is this a private conversation?" Nick asked as he lightly tapped on the door.

My eyes rolled into the back of my head. "How long have you been standing there?"

"Long enough," Nick said, his eyes darting to Jamie for a split second. "I just wanted you to know that I'm not leaving here without you."

Nick was acting like he had something to prove. Maybe he was trying to make up for his past.

"Okay, well, I'm not ready. I don't want to leave Maggie here," I said crossing my arms.

"She'll come around," Nick said with a big smile that went ear to ear.

"It's not just that, I want to make sure we're ready. We need to be ready. Bronx had us pack those bags, which was a step in the right direction, but we didn't know what was out there when we packed them," I said swallowing down the acidic taste at the back of my throat. "I think we need more."

Jamie narrowed his eyes and Nick cocked his head to the side. My eyes moved down to Nick's hip.

"I think we need to be armed. And not with brooms and steak knives." My body shook with my exhale. The words had felt strange leaving my lips. It was something I never thought I'd say.

I could see Jamie staring at me out of the corner of his eye. Clearly, it was something he had been surprised to hear too.

Nick's head bobbed up and down, as he pulled his shoulders back. "You're absolutely right. There's a store not far from here... we can find something there."

"Okay," I said placing my trembling hands on my hips to stop them from shaking.

Nick slowly clasped his hands together in front of his body. "As long as it hasn't all been taken."

ELEVEN

Nick checked his gun while Bronx looked over my assortment of steak knives. Jamie stepped in front of me, his eyes wide as he breathed rapidly.

"I think you should stay here," Jamie said, swallowing as he pressed his lips together. "Your brother and Bronx can handle it."

I grabbed Jamie's arm and pulled him to the side. The feeling of Nick's eyes on us prickled my skin.

"I want to help," I said my voice low as I looked into his eyes. "I want to see what it's like out there."

Jamie dug his fingertips into the back of his neck. "It's just that—"

"It'll be fine," I said with a smile. "We aren't going that far. We'll be back before you know it."

His eyes darted over my shoulder before settling

back on mine. Jamie opened his mouth, but before he could say anything, Nick cleared his throat.

"Ready, Gwen?" Nick asked from the living room.

"Yeah," I said without looking away from Jamie.

I couldn't even understand the thoughts that were going through my head. There was so much in his eyes I couldn't understand, but the one thing I did get was that he was already worried.

There was a slight pinch inside my chest, and I swallowed hard. I forced myself to turn away from him, but he grabbed my hand and pulled me back.

He hesitated and drew in a quick breath. "Be safe."

"Of course." I smiled, and he let go of my hand.

Nick's head was down, but his eyes were on us. As I looked around the room, I noticed he hadn't been the only one watching. Blair had been watching too, and her eyes narrowed when she caught my gaze.

"Let's go," Nick said causing me to turn away from her.

Bronx was standing at the door ready to go. He looked anxious. Excited.

I checked my pocket to make sure I had my apartment key although the others would be here to let us in. It made me feel better to have it just in case.

We stepped out into the hallway, the silence wrapped around me like cling wrap. It felt weird leaving my apartment with Jamie, Blair, and Maggie inside.

Every footstep we took echoed in the hallway. Even though we were trying to be quiet, our surroundings were quieter.

When we got to the bottom of the stairs, we walked down the hall, and into the entranceway. The broken glass crunched under our shoes as we ducked out of the broken door.

Nick carefully looked out toward the parking lot in every direction before waving us forward. The air outside felt thicker, and my heart thumped at the idea that we were surrounded by poison.

It wasn't like my apartment was airtight, so in reality, we were all constantly exposed to whatever was in the air. If there was anything still in the air.

Nick paused and stared at me as if he could tell something was bothering me. I nodded, and he continued leading us through the parking lot.

There were several cars parked in their spots, including mine. Another was stopped half-way in the driveway and half-way in the road. The driver's side door was open. Less than ten feet away there was a body laying on the ground.

The man's eyes were wide, and his body covered in popped blisters. His arm was stretched out over his head as if he'd been reaching for something.

I pinched my nose as the smell found its way to my nostrils. The strong scent of vomit, rot, and death was so overwhelming it made me feel lightheaded.

It wasn't long before I saw another body, and then another. There were so many, I gave up counting.

Each one was in a different position, but most wore the same panicked expression. They didn't know death was coming for them. They'd all been both surprised and in pain.

"Come on," Nick said keeping his voice low as he waved me along. He instantly noticed I was getting distracted by our surroundings. "Try not to look."

"How can I not?" I asked.

"Just try." Nick looked me up and down. "How are you feeling?"

I shrugged. "Fine."

And I did. If there was sickness in the air, it wasn't bothering me. At least not yet. But I didn't feel any better, or worse than I had inside my apartment.

"You?" I asked looking at Nick and then at Bronx.

"Yeah, fine," Nick said, and Bronx nodded.

We walked down the familiar street getting deeper and deeper into the city. Cars were scattered all over the road, likely abandoned when the driver became too ill to keep going. Or as if they'd all stopped working at the same random moment.

Seeing all of the buildings I'd gone past hundreds of times in the empty world made my stomach twist into a knot. They were the same as I'd always remembered, but somehow, they seemed different.

There was trash all over the sidewalk, and if I wasn't stepping over a body, I was stepping over some kind of debris. The city was a mess.

I kept looking over my shoulder. I just couldn't shake the feeling that we were being followed, but every time I looked there wasn't anything there.

"It's just up ahead," Nick said jerking his chin forward.

I'd lived in the area for years and had no idea there was a gun shop in the area. It didn't surprise me that Nick had.

The door to the gun shop was lying on the ground several feet inside the building. The building had been ransacked.

"It's all gone," Bronx said, disappointment in his eyes.

"Seems that way," Nick said, stepping behind the counter. He bent down and went through the cabinets leaving each one open. "Christ."

Bronx was moving things around inside of a broken glass case with the tip of his knife.

"So, what's the deal with you and that guy... Jamie?" Nick asked, keeping his voice low.

"There is no deal," I said narrowing my eyes. "He's a friend."

"Didn't seem that way to me," Nick said raising a brow.

Bronx chuckled. "Me either."

I exhaled slowly trying to keep my breathing steady. "That's all it is. We're friends. Not that it's any of your business."

"Whatever you say," Nick said. He jumped over the counter and landed less than a foot away from me. Nick grinned smugly as he leaned closer. "But just so you know I have eyes."

My teeth pressed together and my jaw muscles tensed. "It's none of your business," I repeated saying each word slowly.

Nick held up his hands and took a step back.

"Okay, okay." Nick turned, and muttered, "but he seems like a fucking pansy."

Bronx chuckled.

"As if you're a good judge of character," I said crossing my arms. My blood was bubbling. Nick always was good at getting on my nerves.

Nick looked as though I'd hit him in the stomach. He'd always thought he was a good judge of character, and that's why he believed he was a good cop.

And he was wrong. Jamie wasn't afraid, he was smart. It wasn't like I knew him well, but he didn't seem like the type that would take risks. He was the exact opposite of Nick, which was why I liked him.

I mean, I liked him in that I thought he was nice. Yeah, he was good-looking, but I had a lot of other things on my mind far more important to worry about.

"Let's get out of here," Nick said turning his back to me. "Waste of time."

"What about this?" Bronx said pulling a long hunting knife out of a light brown decorated sheath.

Nick shrugged. "Better than nothing, but it's not going to save you against a bullet."

"No, no it won't," Bronx said attaching the knife to his pants. "But it's better than a broom."

I glared at him, and he turned away. I was having

instant regrets about coming along with the two amigos. Especially because I hadn't learned anything new about the outside world.

"Is there anywhere else we can check out?" Bronx asked.

Nick tapped his finger to his chin. He was probably mentally going through city maps in his head.

"There are other places, but too far for today," Nick said glancing at me. "Might have to try again another time."

Bronx nodded. "So, when do you think we should leave for your grandma's? I mean if we're planning on more trips out for weapons."

"I don't know," I said before Nick could respond. "We should make sure we have enough packed up, check the bags you had us pack. After seeing those guys... I think maybe my brother is right for the first time in his life and that we need to be prepared."

Nick chuckled.

"Once we're armed and well-rested we should head out," I said staring toward the window. It was odd, but I was almost used to the red glow.

"Are you still feeling ill?" Nick asked, his eyebrows squeezed together with concern.

I shook my head. "No, for the most part, I'm fine, but Maggie still seems exhausted."

"That's more from the loss than it is from the illness," Bronx said lowering his gaze. "They were engaged. Those two were sewn together at the hip. A broken heart for her was probably worse than death."

His words tugged at my heart. I hadn't had anyone like that in my life, but it made me think of losing my mom. The pain was deep. Unrepairable. I could only imagine what Maggie was going through.

"She's a really sweet gal. Tried to set me up with a friend of hers... then all this happened," Bronx said looking down at his feet. He looked back up at my brother wearing a half-grin. "Shit happens, eh?"

"You said it, man," Nick said nodding his head.

"Anyway," Bronx said shifting his weight back and forth. It was like he was trying to shake our eyes off of him. "Should we get back?"

Nick nodded as he walked past him toward the door. He stepped on an old paper coffee cup that crunched loudly under his weight.

"You hear that?" a faint voice whispered from outside of the building.

Nick held his finger to his lip and with the other hand frantically waved for us to get down. I lowered myself soundlessly to my knees behind one of the broken, empty gun cases.

My eyes were so wide, they started to water at

the corners. I looked around hoping a gun would materialize, but the only thing around was broken glass.

My fingers trembled as I reached out for a long shard of glass. I looked out as I leaned to the side, pressing my lips tightly together when someone stepped into view.

TWELVE

I pulled back before he'd seen me. At least I was
pretty sure I had.

I hadn't seen where Nick or Bronx had hid, but if
they were in sight, I'm sure I would have heard by
now. It was one of the men in gas masks that had
been out there, and while I'd only seen one, I was
sure he wasn't alone.

"Came from in there," a man said.

There was a long pause before a loud crunch
filled the air. "You're imagining things. There isn't
anyone in there."

"Yeah, I guess," the man responded in a squeaky
voice filled with uncertainty. He sounded young... a
teenager? "I'm paranoid, you know. God, I hate
this shit."

There was a loud slapping noise followed by a grunt. "Grow a spine, boy. You're going to need it if you plan to make it out of here alive. The world has crumbled, and the only ones that will survive are the strong."

"Yeah, I know. I'm working on it."

"Good boy. Now, let's get back." It was so quiet I could hear the rustling of their clothing as they started to walk away. "We have so much to do."

I didn't move. Even when I couldn't hear their movements any longer, I still hadn't moved.

It was probably a solid twenty minutes before Nick crept over to me. My eyes were filled with panic as I looked up at him, afraid at any second his head was going to get blown off. I didn't like my brother, but I didn't want him dead. And I definitely didn't want to witness his death.

"They're gone," he whispered.

"Are you sure?" I asked.

Nick reached out his hand. "Positive."

I ignored his hand and slowly got to my feet. Bronx was standing near the front of the building, gripping his new hunting knife tightly in his hand.

He looked over at me, and I was sure he could see how much I was shaking. Both he and my brother probably thought I was a pansy too, not that I cared.

"Let's get moving before they decide to come back," Nick whispered.

We darted out of the building and ran down the sidewalk back toward the apartment building. I jumped over bodies and debris. Nick was behind me, but it felt like we were being chased. I was afraid that if I turned around the men in gas masks would be a block behind us, aiming their guns at us.

My breaths were rapid, and it felt like my heart rate was not only fast but erratic. When my apartment building came into view, I didn't relax, even when we stepped inside the entranceway and slightly slowed our pace.

We moved quickly up the stairs. I pulled out my key before we even made it to the door.

The moment I inserted it into the lock, Jamie pulled the door open.

"Jesus, you guys sound like a herd of elephants out there," Jamie said, the happy look on his face quickly falling off his face and being replaced by worry. "What happened?"

Nick pushed past him and quickly closed the door behind us. He locked the door, pressed his back against it, and slid down to his bottom. He was breathing so quickly he couldn't respond.

Jamie turned to me, his eyes wide with long pauses between each blink. "Gwen?"

"Nothing happened," I said between breaths.

"Yeah, sure," Jamie said crossing his arms. After he finished staring at me, his eyes shifted over to Nick's.

"Okay," I said holding up my hand. "Those guys with the masks were out there. They didn't see us."

Jamie narrowed his eyes. "What were you running from?"

"Just running to get the hell back here," Bronx said walking into the kitchen and helping himself to a bottle of water.

Jamie's eyes were back on me. I smiled.

"It's fine. I promise. We just got spooked," I said.

Jamie glanced over his shoulder at Blair and Maggie as if looking for support. "I don't call that spooked."

"How about weapons?" Blair asked, glancing at the new blade at Bronx's hip.

"Everything was gone," Nick said, noticing where her eyes had landed. "Except for that."

"Well, that's not a good sign, right?" Jamie asked.

Nick pushed himself to his feet. "Let's try not to read too much into it. It could just mean we aren't the only ones who want to protect ourselves."

Maggie walked back over to her sleeping area and laid down. She curled up, hugging her knees to her chest as she stared at the wall.

Jamie's his shifted to each of us before jerking his head to the kitchen. My eyes narrowed, and I cross my eyes as I followed him. Nick, Blair, and Bronx were close behind.

"She was like this the whole time you were gone," Jamie said. "Staring. Occasionally whimpering."

"She's been through a lot," Bronx said quickly.

"We all have," Blair said chewing her lip.

Nick held up his hand. He was interested in what else Jamie had to say, or maybe it was because he knew that if we were going to leave, Maggie would have to come with us.

"Of course we have," Nick said, turning to Jamie. "Go on."

"She mentioned something to me," Blair said, glancing at Jamie first. It was like she wasn't sure she should be mentioning it. "She was on medication."

"What kind of medication?" Nick asked, crossing his arms.

Jamie shook her head. "She wouldn't say."

"I think it's for depression or something like

that," Blair whispered somewhat too loudly. Jamie glared at her. "What?"

"We don't know what it was other than it's in her apartment and she refuses to go in there," Jamie said.

"You were going to take her down there while we were gone?" I asked my tone a touch too tart.

Jamie shook his head. "No, of course not. I do wonder if maybe someone should go down there, but after the way you guys rushed in here, I'm rethinking that idea."

"I can hear you guys, you know that right?" Maggie said.

Bronx stepped away from us and over to Maggie. "What do you need? I'll get it for you."

"My prescription," Maggie said dryly. "It's next to the sink. I doubt it'll help anyway."

Bronx looked at Nick. "I'll be right back."

"There, and then right back," Nick said.

Bronx nodded and looked out of the peephole before stepping into the hall. He vanished from sight before Nick had even closed the door.

Jamie pulled me to the side, close to my bedroom and away from the others. He looked me up and down as if checking for something.

"You sure you're okay?" he asked.

I glanced over my shoulder positive Nick was

staring at us. My shoulders relaxed when I spotted him on the sofa with his back toward us.

"Yeah," I said smiling with my eyes as much as my mouth.

He hesitated for a moment before opening his mouth. "What was it like out there?"

"The smell is overpowering, the quiet is terrifying, the feeling that things are lurking in every shadow causes heart-stopping anxiety, but otherwise it was fine." I grinned. "I'm glad to be back inside my apartment."

"Does that mean you changed your mind about leaving?"

I shook my head. "No. I can't." I lowered my gaze. "She needs me."

"Oh, God!" Maggie cried out as she sat up abruptly grabbing her chest.

Nick popped up and was at her side in less than a second. His hands were on her shoulders while his eyes moved over her body, examining her condition.

"My chest!" she cried. "I think I'm dying."

Jamie ran across the room, jumping over my coffee table while I dashed into the kitchen to get her some water.

Maggie was taking in sharp frantic breaths. Her hands clawing at the fabric of her shirt.

"I... can't... breathe," Maggie said, as I knelt down and held out the water. Nick grabbed the bottle and twisted off the cap. He helped her take a sip.

"Take deep breaths," Nick said. He widened his eyes and sucked in a deep breath as if showing her how to do it.

Maggie's eyes locked with Nick's and she followed his lead. She breathed in and out at the exact same times he did. After a few minutes, her hand fell away from her chest.

"There," Nick said, his hand patting her shoulder. "Better?"

"Yes," Maggie said lowering herself back down. "Thank you."

"No problem." Nick's smile showed off his perfect rows of teeth. No doubt grandma had paid for the braces he'd had in his teens. He stood and held out his arms. "Let's give her some room."

Not that I would ever admit it, but I was a little impressed with how my brother handled Maggie. Although she was back to staring blankly.

"Thanks for helping her," I said scrunching my nose slightly at the tangy words.

"Yeah of course," Nick said leaning closer. "Panic attack. Just like mom."

I pressed my lips together remembering the few

I'd witnessed. They'd put Maggie's to shame, well at least this one.

The quick succession of knocks at the door interrupted my thoughts. There was no doubt they came from a desperate fist.

Nick dashed over to the door and peeked out before quickly pulling it open. Bronx stepped inside shaking his head.

"Fuck!" Bronx said, his skin pale. He shuddered when Nick flipped the lock into place. "God dammit!"

Bronx leaned forward placing his hands on his knees. He was working hard to catch his breath.

"I ran up the fucking stairs," Bronx said as if that hadn't been obvious. "Those bastards were outside. The masks."

"Outside?" Nick asked, his eyebrows were squeezed together forming a long caterpillar across his forehead.

Bronx swallowed. "Just outside the entrance."

"Did they see you?" Nick asked as he strode over to the window.

Bronx shook his head. "No... I... I don't think so."

Nick pulled back the curtain slowly, and when he froze, I knew they were out there.

THIRTEEN

I started toward the window, but Jamie grabbed my arm. At the same moment, Nick held up his palm to stop me.

"They're just cutting through the yard," Nick said. "I wonder if they're stationed nearby."

I followed his eyes as they moved over to Maggie. She didn't seem to be paying any attention to what was happening at that moment. Maggie was more wrapped up in what was happening inside her brain.

"We really need to think about leaving soon," Nick said, his voice pillow soft, and his eyes glued to mine. "They're gone."

Nick stepped away from the window and started to pace. I could feel Jamie's body tensing with every passing second.

"Instead of going back out there to look for weapons, how about we check the other apartments," Nick said stopping his feet. He clasped his hands behind his back and rocked back on his heels. "Someone in here must have something."

"It's possible," Bronx said, nodding.

"Sounds safer," Jamie said glancing toward the window. "At least a little."

Nick clapped his hands together, shoving them in his pockets when the sharp noise echoed in the corner of the quiet room.

"There are a few hours of day left, should we go see what we can find?" Nick asked his eyes firmly placed on Bronx.

"Sure," Bronx said straightening his spine. "Let's go."

It was clear I wasn't invited, which was fine because I didn't want to go. I'd had enough excitement for one day.

It wasn't long after they were gone I felt the tension finally leave my body. At least part of the tightness in my muscles could have been blamed on Nick.

I sat at my kitchen table, snacking on crackers while Blair and Jamie sat in the living room. Blair flipped through an old magazine and Jamie was twisting his fingers as he kept an eye on Maggie.

Each bite I took seemed to thunder through the room, but if the others heard it, they made no mention of it. I pushed the crackers away, put my elbow on the table and rested my head down on my fist.

The room was silent except for the occasional rustling of the magazine pages. I started reading the nutritional value on the cracker box for the sixth time.

Both my mind and body were tired, but I wanted to wait for Nick and Bronx to return before excusing myself to my room. The daylight seemed to be vanishing quicker than it had the other days and when I heard the distant rumble of thunder, I knew why.

I walked over to the window and watched the clouds as they rolled in. Maybe the storm would help with the temperature although I was certain my apartment would be stuffy for as long as we were all packed inside.

With the vanishing light, Nick and Bronx would probably be back soon. They wouldn't be able to get much searching done in the darkness.

Jamie caught my eye as I looked toward the door,

and I wondered if he'd had the same thought. With every passing second, I was expecting their knock, but it didn't happen.

Jamie got up and lit the candles. The light danced across his face as he looked into my eyes from only a few feet away.

"They should be back by now," his voice thick with worry.

Blair looked up suddenly interested... and concerned.

"Should you go look for them?" Blair asked. "He is your brother."

"What? No," Jamie said shaking his head. "That's a terrible idea. No one is leaving this apartment."

There was a long silence. Blair didn't look away from Jamie, her expression unreadable.

"They can take care of themselves," Jamie said stepping to the side. "Excuse me."

He walked into the kitchen and turned his back to us. I turned and smiled at Blair.

"He's right. My brother can definitely take care of himself," I said, but my eyes narrowed awkwardly.

He hadn't always been able to take care of himself, but he'd always been strong. And that was mostly what I was referring to because if anything went wrong, he'd find a way to survive.

Lightning struck nearby, and the entire building shook. The floor continued to vibrate as if the strike had caused an earthquake.

Once the light was gone Nick and Bronx wouldn't be able to see well enough to even make their way back. They wouldn't even attempt it.

The only thing we could do was wait.

"I'm going to try to get some sleep," I announced. My sentence punctuated by a bolt of lightning in the distance.

"I can't believe you aren't worried," Blair said, the light caught her judging eyes.

"Who said I'm not worried?" I said standing, trying to keep my hands relaxed even though they wanted to tighten into white-knuckled fists. I opened my mouth to say more but quickly snapped it shut.

I didn't care what Blair thought of me. She didn't know anything about me or my brother.

"They'll be back in the morning," I said through my teeth. Out of the corner of my eye, I could see Jamie watching me. He looked like he was worried he'd have to break up a fight. "That's safer for them than trying to find their way around in the pitch black of the hallways. Now, if you'll excuse me."

I turned on my heel and darted into my room without waiting for a response. Not that she was going to make one, but if she did, I didn't want to hear it.

I wanted to close my door to block her from my view, but with my brother and Bronx missing, I couldn't. Not tonight.

Maybe they'd find a flashlight.

Maybe they'd find their way back, and if they did, I wanted to hear them. I wanted to be able to let them in.

Rain tapped against my window, and instead of soothing me like it used to, it prickled my nerves. I kept picturing the men in masks down in the yard looking up toward the window. I'd only see them when the lightning flashed.

A shiver ran through my body. The candle from the other room didn't offer my bedroom much light. I hated the dark. Always had.

A shadow stepped through my doorway, and for a minute it felt as though my heart had stopped. When I realized it was Jamie, it started pumping once again.

"You can come in," I said when he didn't move.

"Thanks, I just wanted to make sure you were okay," he said standing at the edge of the bed near my feet. "That was a little heated out there."

I tilted my head to the side and twisted my hair between my fingers. "It was? Didn't notice."

"Right," Jamie said with a chuckle.

"I shouldn't let her get on my nerves," I said keeping my voice low.

"She's good at that," Jamie said. Even in the darkness, it looked as though he wished he could take back his words. There was a long pause before he spoke again. "Anyway, I just wanted to make sure you were all right. I'll stay up, you know, just in case."

I shook my head. "You don't have to do that. I doubt I'll be able to get any sleep anyway."

"That worried?"

"An amount." I let out a sigh. "Things are weird with Nick and me, but he's my brother."

The light caught Jamie's half-grin. "I was an only child."

I looked up at him and gave him a smile. For some reason, I didn't want him to leave my room. I didn't want him to leave me alone.

"Well, I should probably get back out there," Jamie said.

"Yeah, sure," I said, but it was the opposite of

what I really wanted to say. I felt better when Jamie was next to me.

"Good night, Gwen," he said tapping his knuckle on the door frame before exiting my room.

A sharp exhale escaped as he walked away. "Good night."

FOURTEEN

When morning came I yawned so hard it pulled a muscle in my neck. My head shot up, and I dug my fingertips into my skin trying to ease away the pain.

I hadn't slept much during the night, and now that there was some light I was sure it wouldn't be long before Nick and Bronx returned. In fact, it was a little odd they hadn't already made their way back. Perhaps the hallways were darker with only the windows at the far ends.

Someone was moving around in the kitchen, but I couldn't quite see who it was. Rather than have to be face to face with Blair, I waited.

My stomach grumbled. With each new day, my

appetite returned more and more. I was pretty sure with how often the others snacked the same had been true for them. There would be more food in the other apartments, but at some point, food might become an issue.

My grandma would have some stored up. She loved to can, not to mention she always had cans of soup and other things she'd buy in bulk. She always said she wanted to make sure she had enough in case she couldn't get into town. This probably hadn't been what she meant.

It had been days since the attack and still there hadn't been any signs of help. Maybe things out there were more widespread than I imagined. Maybe help really wasn't coming.

"Morning," Jamie said passing by my door. "Saw you were awake."

"Yeah, just woke up," I lied.

Jamie's lips curled into a frown. "They're not back yet."

"Oh, yeah I figured someone would have woke me if they'd returned," I said.

Jamie nodded. "Maybe I should go look for them. I mean they're somewhere inside the building, right?"

"No, you shouldn't. They'll be back," I said

forcing a smile. "And if something happened, I wouldn't want it to happen to you too."

Jamie hesitated and then nodded as he returned a smile. "Want something to eat?"

"Definitely." I swung my legs over the side of the bed and stretched my arms over my head. Jamie's eyes were on me but turned away when I looked his way. "Let me change, and then I'll be out."

He nodded and left the room. I looked out of the door before softly closing it behind him.

Maggie had been lying on the floor in the exact same position she'd been in when I'd gone to bed. Blair was in the kitchen wiping the countertop with a paper towel as she snacked on something.

I grabbed a clean t-shirt and jeans from my dressed and dressed quickly. If Nick and Bronx came back, I wanted to be ready.

When I opened my bedroom door, I was hoping to see them standing there, but of course, they weren't there. Blair stepped out of the kitchen and flopped down on the chair, picking up the same magazine she'd flipped through at least seven times.

I walked over to the window and stood next to Jamie. His chin jerked toward the sky.

"I think it's clearing," Jamie said.

The redness did seem as though it had changed.

It was like a bright sunset, only it wouldn't turn into night.

"I wonder if it'll happen again," I muttered.

"What?" Jamie asked.

"Another attack."

Jamie stared at me. "Why would they? They probably think they already wiped everyone out."

"Maybe they'll find out they didn't."

"I guess, but maybe they'll be happy with the massive amount of damage they've already done." Jamie ran his hand through his messy hair. "It could be like this everywhere."

Blair stepped up behind us and placed her hand on Jamie's shoulder. "Try to stay positive. You're always so negative. They're probably organizing help right now."

"If help were coming, it would have been here by now," Jamie said.

"That's not true. They'd need to make sure they didn't get contaminated." Blair's eyes widened. "Oh! Maybe we're in quarantine! Like in the movies."

Jamie shook his head. "If that were the case they'd probably try to get a message to us."

"How would they do that without cell phones?" Blair said scrunching up her nose.

"I don't know they'd find a way," Jamie said.

A quiet noise somewhere in the hallway made us all turn toward the door. Nick and Bronx must have been making their way back to the room.

I tiptoed across the floor and placed my palms against the door as I leaned forward to look out of the peephole. My breathing slowed as I watched for them to step into view.

I blinked several times, waiting and listening. After a long pause, a man in a mask slowly walked past the door.

His eyes were forward. There wasn't anything special about my door that drew his attention, he just kept walking.

It felt like I couldn't breathe. I was frozen in place hoping no one in the apartment would make a noise. Praying to God that Maggie didn't have another panic attack.

When the man was out of my view, a second one made his way past. They walked slowly and softly, but they didn't seem worried about what might be waiting on the other side of the doors.

My heart was racing. I slowly turned and looked at the others over my shoulder holding my shaking index finger to my lips.

There was no doubt they could tell something was wrong.

I turned back to the peephole afraid the bones in my neck might creak too loudly. My eye drew closer to the peephole.

I covered my mouth with my hand when I saw the masked man staring at my door. The doorknob jiggled.

He couldn't see me. There was no way he could see me.

"What about this one?" he asked.

Faint mumbles made their way through the door, but I couldn't make out what he'd been told. The man leaned closer to the door, but then backed up and turned down the hall in the same direction the other two had gone.

I closed my eyes, but other than that I didn't move a muscle. There was no way to tell where they were... maybe they were still out there, or maybe they'd gone.

I'd probably held my position for at least ten minutes when I heard someone behind me. Jamie was standing there looking at me, worry pouring out of his eyes.

My lip quivered, and I leaned toward him, pressing my cheek against his chest. I was about to pull away, embarrassed at my reaction when his arms wrapped around me and squeezed me tighter to him.

I pulled back and looked up at him, his eyes locked with mine. After I blinked, his gaze shifted down toward my lips. His head inched closer, but when I saw Blair waving over his shoulder, I pulled back.

The concern in Jamie's eyes changed to confusion. I jerked my chin toward Blair who was pointing toward the window.

Jamie's comforting arms fell away, and he turned toward the window. I followed as he made his way closer.

He leaned forward peeking out at the side of the window, and I looked out the other side. Down in the yard were the three men with gas masks walking away from the building.

"Jesus," I said sucking in a deep breath. My lungs had craved a full breath. I pointed at my apartment door. "They were out there. In the hall. Right outside our door."

Maggie perked up slightly.

"What were they doing?" Blair asked.

"No idea," I said shaking my head. "He was right on the other side of our door, turning the knob, then he walked away."

"Are they gone?" Maggie asked sounding almost as if she were intoxicated. I glanced at her pill bottle on the floor near her and wondered if she'd taken more than she'd been prescribed.

"Yeah, they're gone," Jamie said.

Blair wrapped her arms around her middle. "What if they come back? I wish your brother and Bronx were here. I feel a lot safer with them around."

It took everything I had not to roll my eyes at her. If Jamie was offended by her remark, he gave no indication.

"Well?" Blair asked tapping her foot. I looked down at it, and she stopped the noise.

"Well, what?" I asked.

She shook her head from side to side. "What if they come back?"

"I... I don't know," I said swallowing hard.

Blair cocked her head to the side. "That's why I wish your brother was here."

I turned away from her before I found my words. Telling her where to go wasn't going to do any of us any good.

It wasn't like Nick had the answers. The only thing he had was a gun, and that probably wasn't going to beat out the three masked men who were more heavily armed than he was.

There was always a chance that the men in gas masks didn't care about us. Yes, it had seemed as though they'd shot that other man but he hadn't looked well. Maybe they'd put him out of his misery.

Not that it was their choice to make. I nervously combed my fingers through my hair.

There was always the chance the men would do something if they found us. One thing I knew for sure was that I didn't want to find out.

My body shook when someone pounded on the door. None of us moved.

FIFTEEN

Jamie and I stared at one another afraid of what was on the other side of the door. Whoever was out there pounded again, harder... desperate.

The men in masks hadn't knocked. They'd turned the knob and tried to come inside.

I soundlessly dashed across the floor and pressed my face to the door. Nick and Bronx were out there each looking down opposite ends of the hall.

I unlocked the door and pulled it open. They both practically fell into the room, breathing heavily.

"Are you okay?" I said bending over, placing my hands on Nick.

"We're fine," Nick said holding up his hand. "We're... fine."

"Where were you?" I asked, looking back and forth between the two men. "What happened?"

Nick stood and wiped the sweat off his brow. "Those fuckers happened."

"They'll be back too," Bronx added.

I shook my head.

"They're working to clear out every apartment in the building. Bringing stuff back to their base," Nick said. "We overheard them talking when we were hiding."

"What took you so long to get back?" I asked.

Nick huffed. "They worked until it was dark. Left with their flashlights. We couldn't even attempt to come back here, and then they were back at it before we could leave."

"The only reason we're here now is because they decided to take a break," Bronx said. "They're clearing the first floor, and then I'm sure they'll come up here."

"They were up here," I said scratching my elbow.

Nick turned sharply. "What do you mean?"

"They passed by the room. Then we saw them in the yard," I said.

"*I* saw them in the yard," Blair said as if making that distinction was important.

"Do they know you're up here?" Nick asked.

I shook my head. "I don't think so."

"Did you hear them say anything else?" Jamie asked.

"Not much. Their base is nearby, they're gathering shit, but other than that they worked rather quietly," Nick said, turning to me. "We're going to have to get out of here. I really don't think it's safe here."

"We don't know anything about them. Why are we just assuming they're bad guys?" I asked.

Nick's mouth dropped open. "You heard what happened to that guy. I don't want that to happen to you, me, or any of us."

"We heard a gunshot, we don't know if they killed that guy. Maybe they brought him back to their base or whatever," I said, but I didn't believe the words. Deep in my gut, I was nearly certain the men had shot that guy even though we hadn't seen it.

"Sure, anything is possible I suppose, but it's not really a risk we should take. Those weapons they're carrying are serious shit. Probably not even something they got from the gun shop down the road," Nick said.

My eyes shifted over to Maggie. She'd barely moved since they'd been back.

I leaned closer to Nick. "We can't just leave her

here. Besides, we're not ready. Did you find any weapons?"

"Just more steak knives," Bronx said.

"If we get out of the city," Nick said pounding his fist to his palm.

"*If?*" Jamie said with a snort.

Nick glared at him. "*When* we get out, we won't have to worry about them."

"Maybe we should just take what we have and get out of here," Bronx said with his hands on his hips. "We packed up a good amount of food and water."

I stepped back away from the group. The intensity and desperation weren't allowing my thoughts to come together to form a cohesive thought. Everything in my mind was a jumbled mess.

"Okay," I said crossing my arms. "There are still things we need to get in order."

"Like what?" Nick asked.

"You weren't here when we packed up, you should find a bag and fill it before those guys take everything of use," I said twisting my fingers together.

Nick's head bobbed up and down quickly. "I can do that. Is that it?"

"Maggie," I whispered, swallowing hard.

"I'll talk to her," Bronx said.

Before he could step away, the wind picked up and slammed the branches of the nearby tree into the window. The wind howled and screeched, and the window rattled.

I walked over to the window and carefully peered out. The dark maroon colored clouds hung low as they sped through the sky.

"A storm," I said jumping back when the branch whipped into the window in front of me. It looked like gnarled fingers reaching out for me. "A big one I guess."

The treetops danced around ferociously bending this way and that. Nick looked out the other side of the window, I could see the red sky reflecting in his eyes.

"This looks like the kind of storm when they usually tell you to go to your basement," Nick said.

"There is no basement," I said, not that it would have mattered. We wouldn't have gone if there had been. "We should probably stay away from the windows."

Nick nodded, but he didn't step back. "Definitely."

I sighed as I turned away from the window. Bronx was sitting next to Maggie, talking softly to her. She had her back to the wall, and her knees pulled up close to her chest. It didn't look as though she were listening to whatever it was he was saying.

Rain started to pound against the window as I walked toward the kitchen. It was crazy how I hadn't realized how small my apartment was before this point.

"Holy shit," Nick said, looking at us over his shoulder. There was a fear in his eyes I hadn't seen before.

"What?"

"Funnel cloud," Nick said pressing both of his palms to his head.

I charged back toward the window and moved the curtain back without thinking. It wasn't very likely that the men in gas masks would be down there during a storm like this anyway.

Debris was flying through the air as the twister ripped through the city. When I saw a car fly through the air and land in our backyard, I knew we were in trouble.

"Away from the window!" I said waving my arms frantically.

Nick grabbed my arm. "Hallway?"

"I don't know," I said shaking my head.

I grabbed Jamie's hand and pulled him into the kitchen. He copied me as I ducked down behind the island.

The others squeezed in on either side of us just as the building started to shake. Jamie wrapped his arm over my shoulder and tilted me forward, setting his body slightly over mine.

Noises of things crashing outside caused my body to shudder and shake. With each noise, I thought the building was going to collapse.

Blair stood and screamed when a painting fell off the wall. Nick placed both hands on her shoulders and held her down. The wind was so loud I could barely hear him as he tried to calm her down.

It sounded like a plane was about to crash into the building. Something inside another apartment made a loud noise, and it felt as though the building was going to be sucked into the earth.

And then it stopped. As quickly as it had approached, it was gone.

We all stayed still, afraid it would start all over again if we moved.

"Stay here," Nick said squeezing Blair's shoulders before he stood. "I'll check it out."

We all stood, but none of us moved out of the

kitchen. I stared at Nick as he cautiously walked across the floor toward the thankfully still intact window.

"Jesus Christ," he said, raking his fingers through his hair. "Its... its...."

We all made our way over to the window. Blair dug her fingers into Bronx's shoulder as she followed him.

Instead of competing for a view at my living room window, I turned toward my bedroom pulling Jamie along with me. We peeked out between the slats of my blinds, and I couldn't hold in my gasp.

The yard was a mess. There were random pieces of wood and metal debris covering the yard. A tree had been uprooted and apparently thrown into the building. The tree that had been near my window had crashed into the side of the building and looked as though it had caused some damage.

"We're going to check out the building," Nick said from just outside my bedroom door.

"I'm coming with you," I said stepping away from Jamie. I didn't glance back in his direction because I knew he'd try to stop me.

"We'll be right back," Nick said to the others as he peeked out of the peephole.

I reached into my pocket and checked to make sure I had my key. We stepped into the hallway and froze before we'd even had a chance to close the door.

The far end of the apartment building where Jamie's apartment had been wasn't there any longer. Wood boards stretched out across the hallway, but between them, I could see the red sky and the rain as it fell down in heavy sheets.

"Let's take a look that way," Nick said jerking his chin over my shoulder.

I'd rarely gone down that end of the hallway. When I'd left the building, I always walked past Jamie's apartment, down the stairs, and out to the parking lot. Now, there was no way to get through.

The floor seemed to squeak loudly as we crept down the messy hall. There was so much scattered junk I could barely find a square of the patterned carpet. It was like all the building materials from the destroyed end of the apartment were sucked into the building.

I followed Nick down the stairs to the first floor. The exit I'd almost never used was blocked by a tree, and I could already see down the hall that the damage on the other end had been extensive.

It hadn't just been the end of the hallway by Jamie's apartment that had been destroyed. It was the whole side of the apartment.

There was no way out.

SIXTEEN

J amie scratched the stubble on his chin. "This is good though right? That also means there's no way in."

"I still want to get to my grandma," I said softly, avoiding his eyes.

"Yeah, I know, but we can take our time and prepare first," Jamie said.

Bronx crossed his arms in front of his broad chest. "We're nearly ready."

"What about weapons?" Jamie asked.

Nick shook his head. "Now that we're trapped inside that doesn't seem likely. Unless we can find something in the remaining apartments, but honestly, I don't know how safe this building is. I'm not sure we should be wandering around."

"You know," I said, smacking my hands down on the kitchen counter, "I could really use a mental break from all of this. I'm freaking exhausted. Can we figure this out later?"

The silence that filled the room chilled my spine. They all stared at me, and all of the eyes focused on me pinched my nerves.

"I'm sorry," I said releasing a breath, hoping they'd turn away. "We've kind of all been through a lot. I just need to gather my thoughts."

I stepped around Bronx and walked toward my room. Without looking, I knew all their eyes were still on me. I could feel it.

"I'm sure grandma is fine," Nick said as I stepped in my doorway. "Storm was miles away from her."

"Maybe I'm not fine," I said, and I closed the door behind me.

My room was dark, with the faint hue of red splashing against my walls. The worst of the storm had passed, but the clouds still covered the sky. Rain was still coming down, showing no signs of easing up.

First, I sat down on my bed, but when that didn't relax me, I laid down. My body was so tense every muscle ached.

The more I tried to relax, the tighter everything

felt. My head hurt, and if it hadn't meant going into the other room, I would have taken some headache medicine. But getting up and going out there would have only made everything tighten up more.

I wasn't sure how much time had gone by, but I was startled by a light knock at the door. I sat up wondering if I had dozed off.

"Yes?" I said my voice a little rough.

"Hey," Jamie said peeking his head inside. "I was just wondering if I could get you anything. You skipped dinner."

"I did?" My room was pitch black except for the small amount of candlelight coming in the doorway.

A muscle in my neck twitched, and I winced. I tried to rub away the pain, but it only pulled the muscle harder.

"You okay?" Jamie asked in a soft voice as if worried the others might hear his question.

"Kink," I said, digging my knuckle into my flesh.

"Here, let me help," Jamie stepped into the room, leaving the door open a crack to allow the light inside.

He sat down on the bed necks to me, his hands warmed my skin as he slid them over my shoulders. My body didn't relax under his touch if anything it made me even more tense.

"Relax," he said softly into my ear.

"Sorry, I'm trying... I've been trying." Fingertips dug into the knot in my neck. "Oh, right there."

"Here?" he asked, and I nodded. My head tipped back, and my body felt like jelly.

"Yeah, that's the spot. That's amazing. Where did you learn how to do that?"

Jamie chuckled. "I pulled a lot of muscles lifting heavy boxes."

"You're supposed to lift with your knees." The words floated out of my mouth like little fluffy clouds.

I could feel Jamie's breath lightly dancing across my neck. It felt cool against the warmth of my skin.

I turned slightly, and his hands stopped. Our faces were inches apart. Everything inside me tensed up again although this time it wasn't painful.

His eyes were on my lips and mine on his. He wasn't moving, but I wanted him to kiss me.

"A-hem," Nick said, as he pushed open the door.

Jamie backed away and folded his hands in his lap. His back was stiff. All traces of the moment popped like a pin to a balloon.

"Oh, hey sorry," Nick said. "Was just checking in. Wanted to see if I can get you anything."

"I'm fine," I said pressing my lips together. "You don't need to worry about me. It's my apartment."

"Right, sorry. Just worried about my little sister you know," Nick said tapping the door with his knuckle. "I'll let you get back to it then. Door closed?"

The knot in my neck instantly returned as did my headache. I should have known that it wasn't from what I'd gone through, it was because of Nick.

"Just go, Nick," I said, and Nick closed the door tightly leaving Jamie and me in the complete darkness. I turned toward him, but I wasn't sure I was looking at him it was so dark. "I'm so sorry about that."

"It's fine." The bed squeaked as he got up. "I should go."

"You don't have to," I said reaching out, but grabbing nothing but air. "My brother is an ass."

Jamie chuckled, and I wished I could see the little wrinkles by his eyes. "Well I'm not going to argue with that, but I really should get back out there."

"Oh, okay," I said hoping the disappointment I was feeling hadn't been noticeable in the tone of my voice.

I wasn't even sure why I was feeling disappointed. There were so many other things I needed to be worrying about. I wasn't even sure I understood what exactly I was feeling for Jamie.

All I'd known was how badly I wanted him to kiss me. It was apparent he hadn't felt the same. He simply cared about me the same way he'd care about anyone he'd considered a friend.

"Hey," Jamie said touching the side of my head in the darkness. "There you are."

His hand slid down my shoulder until he found my hand. He pulled me to my feet.

"This is hard for me to say, but if things were different... it's not right for us to be in here, and them out there, no matter how badly I wanted to kiss you."

My chest squeezed inward as my breath caught in my throat. I felt him inching closer. I could feel his warmth even though our bodies weren't touching.

"But we can't hide out in here, while everything falls apart out there," Jamie said.

I swallowed hard trying to find the right words to say. But I couldn't find them.

"We don't have to hide," I said taking a step forward, stopping when my body touched his.

"It's complicated."

"It doesn't have to be," I said, looking up, struggling to make out the outline of his face.

Jamie's body stiffened, and then I couldn't feel him anymore. I heard him as he felt around the room searching for the door.

"Are you sure I can't get you anything?" he asked as the door opened allowing the light back inside. His face was angled down, refusing to look at me.

"I'll get something myself," I said hugging my middle as I turned away.

"Okay, well if you need anything just let me know."

My jaw stiffened. I turned back to tell him I could take care of myself and that I didn't need him or Nick worrying about me, but he was gone.

SEVENTEEN

I could hear Bronx and Nick talking in the kitchen. They were discussing going through the bags to make sure we'd have everything we needed. After they'd carefully go through the apartments, they could gather up any last-minute items.

When we were ready, we'd break a window and head out to my grandma's. Nick was making plans without me. Without input from any of us. I wasn't at all surprised.

I sat up on my bed and leaned forward until I could see them in the kitchen. I was surprised when Jamie leaned forward resting his palms on the edge of the counter.

"What about Maggie?" Jamie asked.

"We had a good talk, and she says she's ready whenever we are," Bronx said.

Nick's voice was soft. "Now we just need to convince my sister."

I exhaled slowly. If Maggie was truly ready, then I guess it was time to go.

Maybe I'd been making excuses. Even though I wanted to go, I was afraid of what it was going to be like. Hidden inside my apartment just felt safer.

With what happened between Jamie and me, I was ready. At least I would be ready once we were sure we had everything we needed because it was still going to be a long walk. It was probably safe to bet that none of us had ever walked seventy-five miles before.

It would be better at my grandma's, but I was worried about the part in between. Once we got far enough away that I didn't have to worry about the men in gas masks, things would be okay.

After my awkward moment with Jamie, I just wanted to get away. He probably thought I was a desperate loser with how I'd acted.

I tried to shake the memory from my head as I closed the door to change. Might as well go out there and let them all know I was on board.

Nick and Bronx were already going through the

bags when I stepped out of my room. They hadn't even seemed to notice me standing there watching them.

After a few minutes, Nick must have caught a glimpse of me out of the corner of his eye. "Oh, hey sis, we're just double checking our supplies."

"I heard," I said, as I loosely crossed my arms in front of my chest.

"How much did you hear?" Nick stood.

"Probably most," I said taking a quick glance over my shoulder. Maggie was curled up on the floor staring into space. "You sure she's ready for this? It's a long walk. A really, really long walk."

Bronx nodded. "Getting away from here will help."

"She said that?" I asked softly.

"She did," Bronx said looking up at me as he zipped a bag. He stood up and came over to me. "I think getting away from this place will be good for all of us. And not just because it could crumble to the ground at any moment."

Bronx was probably right, and he hadn't even seen the condition of the building.

"Okay, so what's next?" I asked.

"We're going through our things, then we'll check the remaining apartments for any last-minute items," Bronx said. "Then we'll head out in the morning, right Nick?"

"That's right," Nick said without looking away from the bag he was digging around inside of. The bag I'd packed.

My jaw stiffened. "Anything I can do to help?"

"We're good, thanks," Nick said zipping up my bag and moving over to the next. He finally looked up at me. "You should eat something and then rest up. Long journey."

I walked away, making a note to recheck my bag after he left. It wasn't that I didn't trust Nick, but, yeah it was totally that. I'd want to be the last to check over my bag to make sure I had everything I needed. That wasn't something I was going to leave in Nick's hands.

After an hour or so, they left. My mouth dropped when Jamie walked out of the door with them.

He hadn't said a word to me the entire morning. In fact, he hadn't even looked in my direction. Somehow, without even trying, I managed to make a mess of whatever it was that was going on between Jamie and me.

But I just needed to put it behind me. It wasn't like there had really been anything.

I flopped down on the sofa, pushing the blanket

Jamie had been using to the side. I rested my head on my fist and sighed.

"Is that about Jamie?" Blair asked with a smirk.

"Sorry?" My eyebrows squeezed together.

"Your sigh, was that about Jamie?" Blair set down the book she'd been reading. "He's like really moody."

My spine stiffened, and I shook my head. "Oh no, it wasn't."

"Yeah, I bet it was."

I rolled my eyes, and they landed on Maggie who was still in the same position. Her eyes were closed and her breathing shallow. Her bottle of pills was on its side near her hand, several of the little tablets were sprinkled out onto the floor.

"He can be really sweet though," Blair said with a softness to her face.

"How long were you two together," I asked wishing I could take the words back.

Blair grinned, clearly excited to get to talk about herself. "Not long, and it wasn't like official. We were more casual if you know what I mean."

Sadly, I did. My stomach swirled.

"There's nothing going on between Jamie and me," I blurted.

"Well," Blair said cocking her head to the side, "I

see how he looks at you. There could be something going on. You just have to know—"

"Have you seen what's going on out there? I'm not the least bit concerned about starting anything between anyone at this point in time," I said, and it was mostly the truth. Of course, if something with Jamie would have happened, like a kiss, I definitely wouldn't be regretting it.

Blair shrugged and picked the book back up. "Whatever. I was just offering you some friendly advice."

Friendly advice? That was probably the last thing I'd ask Blair for. If I needed anything from Blair, it would probably be lip balm, and I probably wouldn't want to risk sharing that with her either.

"Excuse me," I said as I pushed myself off of the sofa. She already had her nose back in the book before I'd even taken a step toward the kitchen.

Maybe my stomach wasn't twisting because I'd been talking to Blair, maybe I was just hungry. I need to fuel up. Rest. I wanted to be ready.

Not to mention it would probably be good for me to spend as little time as possible with everyone because before I knew it, we'd all be out there. Together. Not a minute of alone time.

After I ate, I rested in my bedroom. I stared at

the window and listened to the rain as it tapped against the glass. The rainstorm was never-ending.

Several hours later, the guys returned. They hadn't brought back much, but Nick was carrying his own backpack. He grinned as he showed me a flashlight.

"Good find," I said.

"Found some batteries too," Nick said, smiling as if he'd won the lottery. "We'll be all set come morning."

"Sounds good," I said trying to match his excitement, but he wasn't buying it.

He walked over to me and placed his hand on my arm. "Can I talk to you for a second?"

"Sure."

Nick led me into my bedroom and closed the door.

"What's up?" I said crossing my arms.

"I wish I didn't have to say this but, you know there's a chance grandma didn't make it, right?"

I let out a long, heavy breath, filled with both annoyance and sadness. "Of course I know that, but there's a chance she's fine, and if she is she's probably scared."

"Grandma? Scared? I doubt that," Nick said,

tilting his head to the side. "She's the toughest woman I know."

"Wonder what she'll think about seeing you after all this time," I said chomping down on my cheek.

Nick's smile faded, but only slightly. He didn't want me to see that my words had hit a nerve.

"Hopefully, she'll be happy to see me. I'll be happy to see her," Nick said with a nonchalant shrug. He might have been playing it cool, but I wasn't buying it. Deep down, he cared what grandma thought.

"Is that all you wanted? To remind me that grandma may not have survived the attack?" I asked.

"Yeah, and to tell you that I was wrong about Jamie."

I narrowed my eyes. "Wrong in what way?"

"He seems like a pretty decent guy."

"Well, I'm glad you think so, I guess." I turned away.

"Um," Nick said drumming his fingers on the wall. "Well, get some rest. Big day ahead of us."

I pasted a smile on my face and turned to him. "Same to you. Same to all of us."

"I'll remind the others too," Nick said as he stepped out of my room.

I didn't stay and get rest, I followed him back out

to the living room, where we all sat together. Nick told stories about when he'd been on the police force. I tried to pay attention, but I zoned out, knowing the stories were probably likely embellished.

My thoughts wouldn't stop shifting to my grandma. I knew the possibility existed that she'd gotten sick and hadn't made it, but I had tried to push those thoughts deep down.

With the number of bodies I'd seen scattered around, I knew the survival rate was low. But it wasn't like I wanted to find her like that.

Either way, we'd be safer out there, and her home probably wasn't about to collapse. It would be a nice place to wait for help... if help was coming.

EIGHTEEN

In the morning, Nick was standing at the living room window. Blair was reading her book, and the others were slouched over.

"We're not going?" I asked.

Only Bronx acknowledge my presence. "Still raining. It's really coming down out there too. We've postponed."

I nodded and walked into the kitchen to grab something to eat. My trash was nearly full, stuffed with empty boxes of food. We'd packed the bags, but we hadn't packed what was on my shelves.

I grabbed a spoon and a jar of peanut butter. The nutty flavor wafted into my nostrils, and my stomach rumbled. My mouth was watering before my tongue even touched the thickly coated spoon.

Blair stood up and walked over to Nick. She placed her hand on the outer side of his shoulder and slowly slid it down over his bicep.

"Can I get some of that?" Bronx said, standing next to me. I hadn't even heard him approach.

It took me a second to realize he was talking about the peanut butter. "Oh, yeah, help yourself."

Bronx opened the drawer and took out a spoon. He dug it into the jar and pulled out a big scoop before leaning back against the counter.

"I packed several jars into my backpack," Bronx said.

"Good." I smiled, but I hadn't been able to draw my eyes away from Blair.

Bronx leaned in closer. "Try not to let that bother you."

"What? Bother me?"

"Yeah, that's just how she is. She's harmless."

"Oh, um," I said with a chuckle. "My brother is like that too, and honestly, Blair doesn't even come close to being his worst choice."

A small laugh rumbled deep inside of Bronx. "I came over here to ease your mind, but now I'm wondering if I should go rescue Blair."

Blair flipped her hair to the side and laughed at something Nick had said. He looked at her over his shoulder wearing a grin. My eyes shot up toward the ceiling, and I turned my back to them.

"Ick," I groaned before scooping out another spoonful of peanut butter. "Do you have anyone out there you'd like to find?"

Bronx looked into my eyes and blinked twice. "I wasn't expecting that question."

"Oh, I'm sorry, I didn't mean to pry."

"It's fine, just caught me by surprise. My dad is stationed out of the country, and my brother, well he can rot in hell for all I care." Bronx said shifting his eyes back toward the living room. "He makes your brother look like a saint."

I shook my head. "You don't know anything about my brother."

"You're right, sorry," Bronx said looking into the jar. "I shouldn't have said that."

"It's fine. It's just a touchy subject."

Bronx leaned closer. "Maybe someday you'll tell me about it."

"Maybe someday you'll tell me about your brother," I said cocking my head to the side as if daring him.

"Someday." Bronx lightly jabbed me with his elbow and grinned. "But not today."

I chuckled. The smile on his face was contagious.

Bronx was very good-looking. I'd thought so since the moment I'd laid eyes on him. It had been his personality that had rubbed me the wrong way, but he was being quite pleasant. He was easy to talk to.

I felt comfortable around Bronx. My body wasn't all tensed up like it was when I was next to Jamie.

Bronx dark eyes were like warm melted chocolate, silky and inviting. His gaze wrapped around me and made me feel like things were going to be okay.

"What was your life like before all this chaos?" Bronx asked taking another scoop.

"It was a different kind of chaos. I'd lost my job. I wasn't even sure how I was going to pay my rent."

"Seems like you won't have to worry about that now." Bronx flashed me a smile that soothed my soul.

I narrowed my eyes playfully. "Is that the bright side?"

He chuckled again.

"I'm not sure there is a bright side to any of this," he said shaking his head. "But if there is, I sure as hell hope we find it."

"Me too," I said, but my life hadn't been the kind to have a whole lot of bright sides. My life had been full of thick dark clouds floating overhead working hard to block out any glimmer of light.

"I should probably stop myself before I eat the whole jar," I said offering the jar to Bronx.

He held up his hand. "No thanks, if I eat any more I'll turn into a peanut."

I screwed on the lid, but the scent of peanut butter still cut through the air. I reached in front of Bronx for my water bottle, and he looked down into my eyes.

"Excuse me," I said feeling a lump in my throat as I pulled back. I took a long drink from the bottle and shifted my gaze to the empty bottles in the trash. "Can we refill those with rainwater?"

Bronx shook his head. "I don't think it would be safe to drink considering we don't know what was, or still is in the air."

"Right," I said with a frown. "I'm running low."

"Not yet we're not," Bronx said, turning and opening my fridge. He pulled out two jugs of water. "Found these when we were out."

"Why are they in the fridge?"

He tucked them back inside. He took a step closer and raised his brow. "Where else does one store water bottles?"

Bronx held out his hand toward me. I stared at it as if it was the first time I'd seen one.

"Join me in the living room?" he asked.

"Sure," I said smiling as I took his hand.

He led me to the empty sofa and pushed aside Jamie's blanket. Jamie was pacing near the window, he stopped for a second before starting back up.

Bronx and I sat down at the same time. I folded my hands into my lap and twisted my fingers together.

Nick turned and looked at us. A smile stretched across his face as he stepped away from the window. He sat down in the chair, and Blair stood behind him, placing her hands on the back of the chair.

"Isn't this nice?" Nick said crossing his legs as his hands slid down the armrests. "All of us together."

I tried to control my breathing as I looked into his empty eyes. It took every ounce of my remaining strength not to get up and go hide in my bedroom.

"Should we go over the plan?" Nick said. "Since we're all together?"

"Whatever you want to do," I said.

"Sounds like a good idea," Bronx said slapping his palm on his knee.

Nick pressed his lips together and steepled his fingers. "Have a seat, Blair. Oh, and Jamie, would you like to join us?"

Blair sat on the floor near Nick's feet. She

crossed her legs and looked up at him batting her eyelashes.

Jamie sat down on the sofa next to me without looking in my direction. Nick started talking, but I couldn't pay him any attention. Blair hung on his every word, and that only annoyed me more.

I sat there, pretending to be paying attention until the sun went down. When I yawned, my brother stopped talking.

"I guess I'm boring you all," Nick said.

"Oh," Blair pouted. "Of course not! You have the most interesting stories. I could listen to you talk all night long."

I rolled my eyes as she blinked up at him like a strobe light. If only it would have been darker, he wouldn't have seen my eyes circling their sockets.

"My sister is getting tired it seems," Nick said patting Blair's hand. "I think if I say another sentence she might fall asleep right there on the sofa."

I was tempted to tell them all that the majority of his stories were fiction colored by an assortment of drugs he'd taken, but I didn't see a reason to ruin their story hour.

"I'm sorry," I said pushing myself to my feet. "Ever since that sickness I just haven't been myself."

It was mostly a lie. For the most part, I was back to feeling like myself.

"I feel great," Nick said.

"Me too," Blair said. "But I don't think I had it all that bad in the first place. I only threw up once."

I shook my head. "You said you felt like you were going to die."

"Well, I did feel that way." Blair blinked rapidly at me. "Sorry I wasn't a vomit fountain like you."

My eyes widened. I couldn't take another second, and I wasn't even sure how I was going to tolerate either her or my brother long enough to make it to my grandma's not to mention the fact that they'd still be hanging around once we got there.

Hopefully, my grandma would put them both in their place. She wasn't going to put up with any nonsense.

"Good night," I said, saluting the room awkwardly.

"Night," Bronx called out.

Nick nodded as I passed by, stepping over Blair's knee.

"Don't forget to get some rest," I said, turning before he could make a snide remark. He must have been tired, or bored because he hadn't even made an attempt.

I lit the candles before disappearing into my room. I left the door open a few inches so I wouldn't be in the complete darkness.

The rain patted against the window, and I shivered. My room was cool, unlike the living room which had felt like the desert in July.

I quickly changed into my sleeping attire, and folded my jeans and t-shirt, setting them on the top of my dresser. As I was about to crawl into bed, I heard my bedroom door squeak, startling me.

I turned sharply and watched Jamie enter my room closing the door nearly all the way behind him. He turned to me, drew in a breath and charged across the bedroom floor.

His hand slid around my neck, and he pulled me close. He pressed his lips to mine, hard. I felt his need like a swimmer gasping for a breath of air before his next stroke.

Jamie's lips softly gliding against mine, as his thumbs brushed my cheeks. My heart raced, and then stopped, only to speed up more.

He pulled back, and all I could do was stare at his lips as my chest rose and fell with each breath. My muscles were tensed again, but it felt good. So damn good.

"What was that for?" My breath was like a bubble floating into the sky.

Jamie's finger glided down my cheek and across my lower lip. My eyes shifted upward, and his hand fell away.

He kissed me again.

NINETEEN

Jamie took a step back, and I shook my head. There he was sending those mixed messages again.

"What was that for?" I asked biting my lip. I could still feel his mouth on mine even though he was several feet away. My body ached for the feel of him pressed against me again.

"I don't know," Jamie said raking his finger through his hair. "It's just that I saw how he was looking at you."

I shook my head. "How who was looking at me?"

"Bronx." Jamie sucked in a breath. "I don't know what the fuck I'm doing. I just keep screwing everything up. Making things worse. I always make things worse."

"You haven't made anything worse," I said, biting my cheek.

"I shouldn't have come in here like that. I'm sorry." Jamie took another step back. "Jesus, I'm such a screw-up."

I took a step forward, and Jamie held up his palm. He shook his head and backed out of the room without another word, leaving me standing there staring at the emptiness he'd left in my room.

I wanted to chase after him. Get answers. But I couldn't because the others were out there, and because I probably would have seemed like a crazy person. Although *I* wasn't the one being a crazy person. Was I?

Maybe he just needed a moment, and he'd be back. He probably had to clear his head. After all, the moment had been intense.

I sat down on the bed, still staring at the door. It didn't take me long to realize he wasn't coming back.

I laid down on top of my blankets trying my hardest not to think of the kiss. But my thoughts always came back to it.

I turned over onto my side with my back to the door, looking at the empty space next to me. Jamie could have been in that space. I could have been lying there gazing into his crystal blue eyes.

Instead, I was lying there wondering what I'd done wrong. One thing I knew for sure was that I had to stop thinking about him. We were going to be spending a lot of time together, and I didn't want things to be any more awkward than they already were.

Jamie and I could be friends. Nothing more. No matter how badly I wanted another kiss, I had to push the thoughts away. It wasn't right. It wouldn't work.

Maybe that's what Jamie had realized. Maybe that's why he'd walked out of the room.

* * *

Strong winds threw the droplets of rain harshly against my bedroom window. Thunder rumbled shaking the floor and my mattress. I sat up worried that my apartment was going to crash down onto the first floor.

It was still dark, but there was a small amount of light, so I knew it must have been close to morning. I could hear someone moving in the living room. And then moments later, a stream of curses.

I hugged myself as I walked into the living room.

Nick must have seen me through the corner of his eye.

"Look at that," he said pointing down at the yard. "That's gotta be several inches of standing water."

I stepped up to the window and shuddered as a bolt of lightning shot out of the sky striking a few blocks away. The electricity rippled through the air causing my skin to prickle.

"It's the never-ending storm," Nick said, disappointment thick in his voice.

I stared at him waiting for him to say what he didn't want to say. He was by far the most anxious to get out of my apartment, and not only because half of it was missing. Nick didn't like the men in gas masks, but we hadn't seen them in days. For all we knew, the tornado had blown them away.

"It's either we put it off another day, or we slosh through the muck," Nick said turning to me.

"The weather will slow us down tremendously. It'll make traveling difficult," I said with a small half-shrug.

"Dammit," he spat. "A strong wind could knock what's left of this place to the ground."

I chewed my lip for a moment. It would probably take more than just a strong wind. But if everyone wanted to leave, I'd join them. Getting out of my cramped apartment was awfully tempting even with the rain pouring down and thunder shaking the earth.

Lightning crashed down a few blocks away, and Nick shook his head. I wondered if he too was starting to feel crowded... maybe it had something to do with Blair. Although I sure as hell wasn't going to ask, and it probably didn't.

"Guess we're here another day," Nick groaned before slamming his palm against the wall. "Sorry guys."

"It's okay," Blair sang in a far too cheery voice.

"Yeah, it's not your fault, man," Bronx said stretching his arms over his head, revealing his muscled stomach.

Nick looked up at me before taking a step closer. He opened his mouth but snapped it shut before walking into the kitchen.

It almost felt as though he wanted to blame me. Maybe he thought that if I would have let us leave sooner, we'd be almost there.

"I'm sure the rain will stop soon. It's not like it can go on like this forever," I said turning toward the kitchen.

Nick was making himself a peanut butter sandwich on bread that was starting to look questionable.

He grunted and took a bite of the sandwich. I walked into the kitchen and stood next to him. His eyes shifted over, but he didn't move his head.

"Why are you so anxious to get out of here anyway?" I asked keeping my voice low.

"Maybe I'm starting to feel a little claustrophobic," Nick said answering quickly. There were droplets of sweat gathered up at his temples. His eyes were shifting around in their sockets.

I cocked my head to the side. "Have you been sleeping at all?"

"Not much," he said shaking his head. "Who needs it?"

He turned to me flashing me a smirk that made my skin crawl. Something wasn't right. His pupils were hugely dilated, and the whites of his eyes were bloodshot.

"God dammit, Nick," I said leaning closer. "Have you been... been using?"

"What?" He released an awkward chuckle that vibrated through his nostrils. The tendons in his neck jutted out as he inched his face closer to mine. "Don't be stupid."

The anger that radiated out of him frightened me, and it confirmed my suspicions. His hand tightened into a fist, and he slammed it down on the counter.

"How dare you even ask me that?" Nick said. The fury that poured out of his bloodshot eyes sent a shiver down my spine.

I ignored my fear and pulled my shoulders back. "Why did you do it, Nick?" Disappointment coated my words. "Where did you even find it?"

He bared his teeth like he was a wild animal. I glanced toward the living room over my shoulder, and Nick's eyes followed mine.

Bronx was staring at us, his eyes narrowed. There was no doubt that even though he couldn't hear us, he was concerned about what Nick and I were discussing.

"Keep your fucking voice down my sweet sister." Nick's tone was as sour as it was salty.

"You wanted us all to follow you out of here, but no one is going to want an addict leading the way. Gun or not," I said crossing my arms.

The knuckles on his fist were paper-white. First, his anger increased, and I thought he was going to pick me up and throw me out of the window, but then his face softened. He looked like he was going to cry.

"I was going to throw it away, I really was," Nick said.

"But you didn't."

"You can't tell them," Nick pleaded.

I shook my head. "Of course I can."

"Look," Nick said, his eyes bulging out of their sockets, "it's gone. It won't happen again. I made a mistake. Everything just got to me."

"If I had a nickel for every time I've heard that."

Bronx stood up, his eyes still on us.

"Please don't tell him," Nick said shifting his weight.

"He can probably tell."

"I'll make this right with you, I promise," Nick said, turning the ends of his mouth upward as Bronx approached.

Bronx looked back and forth between us, settling his eyes on me. "Everything okay here?"

My stomach twisted. I knew what I should have said, but I was an idiot.

"Yeah, we were just discussing which route to take to grandma's," I said hating that I was lying for my brother. "He thinks he has a shortcut, but you pretty much never want to take one of my brother's shortcuts."

Nick forced an awkward laugh. "Aw, they're not

that bad."

"They're terrible," I said taking a step out of the kitchen. I couldn't stand to be next to him, not even for a minute longer. "Excuse me."

I wished I could have left the apartment, but the only place I could go to get away from Nick was my bedroom.

When I stepped into my bedroom, I wanted to punch something. My pillow. The wall. Nick. But I sat down on the bed and drew in several long deep breaths.

I couldn't help but wonder when he'd found whatever he'd taken. How long had he been hiding it before he finally broken down? Not that it mattered, he still took it.

There was a light knock at my door, and Bronx peeked his head inside. I could tell by the look on his face that he knew something was up.

"Sorry to bother you, but your brother wanted me to tell you they're back," Bronx said jerking his chin toward the window.

My stomach started to swirl as I stood up and made my way to the window. When I saw them wading through the flooding and debris, my mouth dropped open.

I really wanted to hit something.

TWENTY

I shook my head after Bronx asked me to come into the living room to discuss things with the group. There wasn't anything he could do or say that would get me out there to discuss what we were going to do while my brother was wasted.

"Shouldn't we discuss this?" Bronx asked. "This changes things even with the rain and storms, doesn't it?"

"They can't get inside," I said with a confident half-shrug.

Bronx looked over his shoulder and shook his head before stepping into the room. "I'm sure they could find a way. Just like we plan to find a way out."

The floor creaked as he took several steps into my room. I didn't turn away from the window.

The redness in the sky seemed to have lessened, perhaps because of the storm. Still, the men wore their masks as they tried to move through the yard.

Water came up to their knees, and it looked as though they were struggling to wade through. It was as though the earth below was trying to suck them down into the soggy ground.

"They're turning back," I said just as Bronx stepped up beside me.

"That's good for now, but not good that they're still out there, and still trying to get to the apartment." I could feel Bronx looking at me, but I tried to ignore it. "He just wants to talk about leaving."

The masked men stepped out of a view, and I turned away from the window. "I can't talk to him right now. Tell him I'm not feeling well."

"You look fine," Bronx said flashing me a smile. "Do you want to talk about it?"

"I definitely don't want to talk about it," I said refusing to meet his gaze.

"I think I know what this is about," Bronx said lowering his voice.

I shook my head and crossed my arms.

"It's about his eyes isn't it?"

My lips pressed together tightly as I cocked my head to the side. "Eyes?"

"Yeah, I think you know what I mean," Bronx said. "Not to mention I was with him when he found it. He thought he was being sneaky but," Bronx said leaning closer, "I see everything."

I blinked several times. "He doesn't know that you saw him?"

Bronx shook his head. "He stared at it for a solid minute before he stuffed it into his pocket. Inner struggles perhaps."

"Why didn't you say something?" I asked wishing I could take the question back. It wasn't Bronx's duty to stop my brother.

"I didn't really know what to say." He tilted his head down. "I guess I probably should have. Has he been using long?"

I glanced at the door and then back at Bronx. "Quite some time. Thought it was done but I guess I was wrong."

"Is that what you two were discussing in the kitchen earlier?"

I nodded. "He didn't want me to say anything to the others."

"I don't blame him."

"So, if you could just keep this between you and me I'd really—"

"Say no more," Bronx said tilting his head to have

a better look into my eyes. "I wouldn't have anyway. He seems like a good guy... we all have our demons, don't we?"

I shook my head as I looked back into his eyes wondering what kind of demons Bronx might have.

"Just tell him I'm fine with whatever he wants to do," I said waving my hand in the air as if I'd seen a mosquito.

"As you wish," Bronx said taking one last look at me as if I might change my mind before exiting my bedroom.

I turned back to the window, but the men were long gone. Hopefully, they wouldn't try again, until the standing water dissipated, and we were long gone.

Soft voices from the other room floated through the air like clouds on a summer day. I moved closer to the door.

Nick was talking. "We're leaving tomorrow unless someone has a good reason not to. Our time here is up."

"I just don't know," Jamie said. "If they couldn't even make it through the yard, how will we?"

"It'll be hard, but we'll find higher ground. I know the best routes," Nick said.

"We should give it a little more time," Jamie said.

"At least wait until the rain stops."

Footsteps tapped against the floor. "We can't keep putting this off," Nick said. "Eventually they're going to make their way back here. We don't want to be here when that happens."

"They gave up. They aren't coming back," Jamie said.

"Maybe not yet, but they will," Nick said his voice rising with each word. I could tell he was struggling to keep himself calm.

Before I knew it, my feet were carrying me into the other room. Nick's eyes shot up.

"That means we still have time," Jamie said turning as he heard me coming up next to him. "Tell him we should give it more time."

I looked into Nick's eyes, studying them. It looked like he was crashing. He was sweating, and his fingers were shaking.

"Nick," I said keeping my voice steady, "I think you need to sleep on it. Take my room."

"I don't need rest," Nick said, his fists tightening. It looked like he wanted to jump out of the window and compete in an iron man competition. "What we need is to get out of here."

Blair wrapped her arms around herself. "If Nick

says we should go, we should probably go. He was a police officer."

"Police officers don't necessarily know how to handle situations like this. No one does," I said. "We don't even know what those guys are really after. They probably just want supplies."

"And they'll fight for them," Nick said.

"Whatever," I said letting out a heavy sigh. "Here's the deal. You sleep on it, and whatever you decide in the morning, I'll support you."

It looked like countless responses were zipping through his mind. I shifted my weight and stared at him, trying to mentally convey that I wasn't going to change my mind.

"Or your other option is to take your bag and go. Anyone that wants to go with him, is more than welcome to leave." I stiffened my jaw. "Don't worry about me. I'll catch up."

Not that anyone had been worrying.

"Okay, so who's with me," Nick said stomping over to the pile of backpacks.

"Me," Blair said looking at me out of the corner of her eye.

"I guess me too," Maggie said with a shrug.

Jamie put his hands on his hips and shook his head. He didn't even have a chance to say his peace before Nick turned to Bronx.

"What about you?" Nick asked.

Bronx ran his fingers through his hair. "Wow," he said with a chuckle. "Nothing like putting me on the spot."

"It's not a difficult question," Nick said his gaze seared Bronx's flesh.

The tiny smile that had been on Bronx's face vanished. "You know what, I think I'll stay back and make sure your sister gets out of here safely."

Nick and Bronx exchanged a heated look. The tension in the room became so thick it was hard to breathe.

"Well, I guess that's all decided then. We'll see you guys soon." Nick shifted his cold glare my way. "You remember the way, right?"

"Funny," I said cocking my head to the side, "was going to ask you the same thing."

Nick clapped his hands, and I shuddered. "Well, are we ready to go ladies?"

Blair raised her nose into the air and stood next to Nick. "Whenever you are, right Maggie?"

"Sure," Maggie said seemingly disinterested.

"Maybe you should wait until morning," I said as

Nick pushed past me heading toward the backpacks. "You'll run out of light soon."

"We have flashlights," Nick said, as he drew a shaky hand under his nose.

I reached out for his shoulder but quickly pulled my hand back before touching him. "With the flooding, don't you think it would be a better idea to just put it off a few more hours? Those men won't come poking around here at night anyway."

"I think she's right," Jamie said.

Nick turned sharply, his shoulders rising and falling. He looked like a wild animal ready to pounce on its prey.

Jamie took a step back and held up his palms. "It was just a suggestion."

"Well, I don't need any suggestions," Nick said as he glanced at the window. His shoulders and expression both softened at the same time. "Maybe I didn't realize how late it was."

"We have the flashlights." Blair shrugged.

"No, no," Nick said placing his hand on Blair's shoulder. "Their right. We should go in the morning. First thing."

I let out a long breath, relieved mostly for Maggie and Blair. But my relief was only temporary because there was no doubt in my mind that they were leaving in the morning. At least I'd feel a little better about Maggie and Blair being with him when whatever he'd taken would be out of his system.

There probably wasn't anything I could say to Blair to change her mind, and I wasn't even sure I wanted to bother. She was a grown woman and could make her own choices. If she couldn't see right through my brother, that was her problem, not mine.

And Maggie, I could tell her everything, and she'd just shrug. She was in her own stupor, one from a prescription that would soon run out.

"Let's eat something and then get our rest," Nick said mostly to Blair because Maggie hadn't moved from her little corner on the floor.

"Great idea," Blair said shooting me a quick glance of superiority.

Nick ate quickly. He doubled checked the lock on my door before stopping to peer out the window. After about five minutes he laid down on the floor and nearly instantly, he crashed.

Maybe, if Blair and Maggie were lucky, he'd sleep right through the entire day.

TWENTY-ONE

I hadn't slept well. My dreams were all about the various ways Nick was going to die. First, the muddy earth swallowed him up, and then in the second dream, poison rained down from the sky. There was another, but it was less realistic and involved trees coming to life.

I was awake before I heard movement in the living room. For a moment I considered not going out there... not saying goodbye to my brother, but I think because of the dreams, I had to. It wasn't like I'd ever wished death upon my brother, all I'd wanted was for things to have been different.

I looked out of the window for a long moment as I listened to whoever was up walking around the apartment. Someone stopped in front of my door, and I glanced over my shoulder.

It was still dark, but there was enough light to see Nick standing there. His breathing was normal. His eyes were still bloodshot, but his pupils had returned to normal. He no longer looked like he was sweating himself into dehydration.

"You're up," he said, stepping into the room. "We're going to head out soon."

"Okay," I said.

"I just wanted to tell you something before we go," Nick said.

My eyes blinked rapidly as I stared at him. "What?"

"I'm really sorry about what happened yesterday," he said, and I could tell he was sincerely sorry. The only problem was that every time he relapsed he'd been sincerely sorry. This wasn't any different. "I really screwed up, it's just that everything got to me. The loss. Being cooped up. The end of the world. I fucked up, and I'm sorry. I know you won't believe me, but it won't happen again."

"Only because eventually you won't be able to find any," I said with a shrug.

Nick shook his head and looked down at his feet. "Well, believe it or not, I really am sorry. And pissed off at myself for being so weak." He covered his mouth and coughed. "Anyway, thanks for not outing me."

"I probably should have," I said tilting my head slightly.

"I appreciate that you didn't," Nick brushed his hair back with his hands. "Are you sure you don't want to join us?"

I shook my head. "Seventy-five miles is far too long to walk through puddles for me."

Nick chuckled. "Don't be too long. I don't want to have to come back here and get you."

"Good luck, Nick," I said with a small smile. It was the most I could offer him. "Take care of Blair and Maggie."

"Of course," Nick said nodding. "And I know you'll be in good hands with Bronx."

I raised a brow wanting to tell him I could take care of myself, but in a way, he was right. I would feel safer with Bronx and Jamie at my side.

"I'll see you soon then?" Nick asked.

"Yes, soon."

He stood there staring first at the floor, and then his gaze shifted up at me. I knew he was considering hugging me. In the end, he decided not to, turned, and left my room.

I stayed in my room. Not wanting to see any of them leave. I probably should have said goodbye to Blair and Maggie, but it wasn't like I'd been close to them. They'd stayed in my apartment, and that was the extent of our relationship.

I listened as they said their goodbyes. When the door closed, I did everything I could to fight back the tears.

My brother may have been a stupid asshole jerk, but he was my brother. There was a fairly decent chance that he was the only family I had left.

But I wasn't going to cry. It wouldn't be long until I saw him again. Hell, if the rain stopped, maybe we'd even catch up to them on the way.

When I was sure I wasn't going to burst into tears, I joined Bronx and Jamie in the living room. Bronx was staring out of the window, and Jamie was pacing near the front door as if he expected them to return.

They both glanced at me at the same moment, but neither of them spoke. The apartment was so quiet without them here that I could have heard a feather floating through the air.

There was a strange muffled squeak that came up through the flooring, followed by the sounds of a window breaking. They must have found a way out or rather made a way out.

"They're in the backyard," Bronx announced his voice sounding particularly loud in the silence. He lowered it significantly. "The water is to their knees."

I walked over to the window and peeked out of the other side. Nick was holding on to Blair and Maggie as they trudged through the water. He was heading in the opposite direction we'd always seen the men coming from.

They moved much quicker than I thought they would through the mucky, murky water. Maybe they were motivated by fear, or maybe they were just happy to be out of my cramped apartment.

"They're really doing it," Bronx said as they approached the far left side of the yard near the tree line.

"I guess so." The exhale that escaped from between my lips resembled a sigh.

"For the record, I think waiting was the right choice," Bronx said.

I shrugged. "Who knows?"

And with that Nick, Maggie, and Blair were out of view. Gone.

Bronx placed his hand on my shoulder briefly

before stepping away from the window. I stared into the yard once again fighting back the tears.

As I was about to turn away the water near the trees started to ripple. Seconds later, Maggie stepped back into view, followed by Blair.

"They're coming back," I said shaking my head. I looked over my shoulder at Bronx. His eyes were narrowed, and Jamie was staring at the window. "Why are they coming back?"

When I turned back to the window, I saw Nick step into view, and he wasn't alone. The floor creaked as Bronx quickly made his way to the window.

One man wearing a gas mask stepped out, and then the other two. All three of the men pointed their big, deadly guns at them. The one closest to Nick had his gun aimed directly at the back of his head.

"Oh my God," I said softly.

Nick's eyes darted up toward the window for a split second. There was no way them men could have seen the look from behind him.

Maggie's arms were wrapped around her middle so tightly it looked as though she was holding herself together. Blair's eyes bulged, and I could tell from our distance that she was crying.

"Help us!" Blair cried. Her voice was faint in the apartment, but it had probably stung the men's ears where they stood.

Blair's eyes shifted up toward the second floor. Apparently, she wasn't sure which window to look at.

One of the men sloshed quickly through the water and stepped in front of Blair. The whole group stopped moving.

I couldn't make out any of the words, but it was obvious the man was shouting something at Blair. He raised his hand and smacked her hard across the face with the back of his hand.

Blair's fingertips flew up to her cheek, and she stared at the man. Her shoulders dropped, and the man pushed his gun between her shoulder blades until she started walking again.

The men led them through the water, off toward the right. For a second the man looked up at the apartment building. I froze, holding my breath. The man's eyes scanned the area and didn't stop on any specific window.

It wasn't long before they were all out of view. My heart was like a bass drum pounding inside my chest echoing down to my feet. I was afraid it was vibrating out of my body and down into the water, giving away our location.

Bronx swallowed hard as he turned me to face him. "We have to go after them."

"What?" Jamie said throwing his hands into the air. "Are you crazy?"

"Not even a little," Bronx said turning sharply.

"Well, you sound like it," Jamie said, his shoulders rising and falling with each quick breath.

Bronx flew across the room and grabbed his shirt at the shoulders. He pressed him hard against the wall as he stared into Jamie's eyes.

"You better watch what you say," Bronx said between his teeth. "Lest you end up with my fist in your face."

Jamie chuckled. He tried to hide the nervousness, but he'd failed.

"You can stay here and be a little chicken shit if you want, but I'm going out there. I'll find them," Bronx said, the veins in his forearms protruded as he pushed Jamie harder against the wall before releasing him.

Jamie rubbed his shoulder. "You don't know where to go, and all you have is that hunting blade. It would be incredibly stupid to put that up against their guns."

"I don't think they're that far, in fact, I think they're much closer than we'd like. A house. A business. The nearby church." Bronx shook his head.

"They could be anywhere," Jamie said.

"Bronx is right," I said after a long pause. "We have to do something. We're all they have left."

Jamie exhaled slowly. "It could already be too late."

"There wasn't a gunshot like there had been with that sick guy," I replied.

"That doesn't mean anything," Jamie said.

"It means there is a chance they're still alive," I said pushing my shoulders back.

Jamie shook his head. "We can't just charge out there stomping through the water, demanding they release them. They'll laugh at us and then shoot us in the face."

"We don't have a lot of choices," I said crossing my arms.

"Hang on," Bronx said holding up his hand. "He's right, but there is something we can do that might actually work."

Jamie and I both turned to him. My heart thumped hard before returning to its quickened rhythm.

"We go at night," Bronx said gesturing toward the backpacks.

Jamie shook his head. "We can't see at—"

"The flashlights," Bronx said. "If we go out at night, we can see which buildings have the lights on."

Bronx looked back and forth between us, the straight line of his mouth almost turned into a smile.

"It's a good idea, right?" Bronx asked.

My lips curled up at the end, and I nodded. Even Jamie looked a little impressed.

"Nick wouldn't want us to attempt this," I said feeling a chill run through my veins.

"No, he wouldn't," Bronx said, raising a brow. "But that's just tough shit. He'd come for us. Maybe even Jamie."

Jamie shook his head. "I doubt it."

Bronx chuckled.

Nick probably deserved everything that was happening to him, but after everything he'd put our family and me through, he was still my brother. He would have come for me, and I would do the same for him.

"I'm in," I said.

"All right then, it's settled." Bronx stiffened his jaw. "Tonight."

TWENTY-TWO

I had changed into a dark t-shirt and pulled on a knit hat. Darkness was falling fast, and it wouldn't be long before we were out there wading through the water in the blackness of the night.

Bronx had the flashlight on the counter next to the steak knives Jamie, and I would carry. The knives that would do absolutely no good against the big guns of the men with gas masks.

I glanced out of my bedroom window before heading into the living room where Bronx and Jamie were waiting. Jamie stopped pacing and looked up at me when I entered the room.

"Planning to rob a bank while we're out?" he teased.

"You're trying to joke around, but someone out there has probably already done just that," I said.

"You're probably right," Jamie said with a chuckle.

Bronx stepped away from the window and stood next to me. "He's just jealous you're appropriately dressed, and we aren't."

"A little." Jamie grinned. "And if my apartment hadn't been ripped off the side of the building, I'd have changed too."

"We could look in some of the other apartments?" I suggested.

Bronx shook his head. "Probably not worth it. Let's get out and get back as fast as we can. Learn what we can."

I nodded.

"I still don't know what we're going to do if we find where they're staying," Jamie said.

"We'll figure something out," Bronx said handing me one of the steak knives as he picked up the flashlight. He jerked his chin sharply to the door. "Got your key?"

"Yeah," I said.

Bronx raised both brows. "Then off we go."

We stepped out into the hall, looking in every

direction as if we expected someone to jump out at us. The silence alone sent a chill down my spine.

I turned and locked the door before following Bronx down the creaky, squeaky hallway. Jamie followed close behind me.

Bronx kept the flashlight aimed low to the ground with his finger on the button. We walked down the stairs slowly, hoping to minimize the noise each step made.

"Hold on," Bronx said as he grabbed the railing. The small beam of light from the flashlight lit up the water that hid the last few stairs.

It ripped softly when Bronx stepped down into the water. A shiver shook his entire body.

"Sheesh, it's cold," Bronx said just as I placed my food down into the frigged flood water.

"Oooh," I whispered as my body started to shake uncontrollably.

The water sloshed as we made our way through. Various unknown things under the surface brushed against my legs. We tried to be silent, but it was nearly impossible.

Personal items from the apartments floated on the surface of the water, moving around as we created waves. We looked into each of the apartments for the window Nick had broken.

Bronx didn't even have to raise the flashlight when we found it, the chilly breeze was enough to give it away. Even though it was still raining, there was a small amount of light in the sky which gave everything a slight glow, enough to see the way out.

"Watch your step," Bronx advised as he clicked off his flashlight.

With each step, it felt like there were things slithering under the surface trying to grab my legs. I took another step, and I couldn't move my foot. The more I pulled, the more it pulled me back.

I reached forward for Bronx attempting to steady myself, but I misjudged my reach and fell forward into the water. My arms splashed around as I tried to get my head over the surface, but whatever had my foot was keeping me in place.

Bronx grabbed me under the arms and raised me above the surface. I frantically gasped for air.

"My foot," I said taking in another breath, "it's stuck!"

I could feel hands moving down my leg, stopping near my ankle. After a second my foot was free, and I was able to stand up.

My heart was still racing as my eyes darted around the water trying to find the wild beast that had attacked me.

"You okay?" Bronx asked.

It felt like I was stuck inside a block of ice. My teeth chattered, and my lips were as cold as popsicles.

"Yeah, yeah," I said wrapping my icy arms around my even colder body. "Freaked myself out I guess."

"Easy to do," Bronx whispered as he took another step toward the broken window.

A light flashed through the broken glass and across the wall just above our heads.

"Get down!" Bronx said, his voice softer than the air. Jamie and I crouched down immediately, but it was less than a second before Bronx started waving us back toward the door. "They're out there! Go back! Go back!"

It felt as though the water was sucking us out toward the window as we fought our way out of the apartment. The light moved through the room again just as we stepped into the first-floor hallway.

Bronx waved his hand toward the stairs. Jamie grabbed my hand and pulled me with him as he led me toward the stairwell.

The water sloshed noisily around us creating waves. I was worried the motion of the water would be enough to give us away.

I looked over my shoulder at Bronx. "Did you see who was out there?"

"No, but I have a pretty good guess," he said placing his hand on my back as we walked up the stairs.

When we got to the top of the stairs, I took one step and water squished out of my shoe. I turned back as we walked looking at the trail I was leaving that would lead them right to our room.

"Shit," I said pulling my hand free from Jamie. He was leaving behind the same wet footprints.

"There isn't anything we can do," Bronx said giving me a gentle push.

I pulled out my keys, my fingers shaking as I tried to put the key in the lock. My nerves and the cold rattled my bones making it impossible for me to line up the key.

"Here," Jamie said, grabbing the key. He expertly inserted it into the lock and opened the door, handing me back my set of keys.

"Thank God the candles aren't burning," Bronx said closing the door softly. He locked it and then put his finger to his lips as he walked toward the window.

I listened hard in the silence. If the men were wading through the water on the first floor, I thought I'd be able to hear them, but I heard nothing.

"I can see them," Bronx said, his eye just at the edge of the curtain.

"What are they doing?" Jamie asked. He hadn't moved from the spot near the front door.

"I think they're doing what we were doing," Bronx said shaking his head. "Looking for lights."

Jamie crossed his arms. "Do you think they told them we're still up here? Are they looking for us?"

"Nick wouldn't do that," Bronx said.

"Blair might," Jamie muttered.

Bronx shook his head. "I don't think she would."

"To save herself? Yeah, I definitely think she would," Jamie said, but Bronx appeared to be ignoring him.

Bronx held up his palm, his eyes wide as he peered out of the side of the window. "Get her in her room, stay there until it's safe to come out."

"What are they doing?" I asked my eyes glued to the curtain wishing I could see through them.

"Studying the building," Bronx said barely moving his lips. "Thoroughly. It looks like they're looking for something... someone. Hopefully, when they don't see any light, they'll move on."

"Come on," Jamie said placing his hand on my shoulder.

I nodded and turned toward my room. The steps we took were slow and careful... nearly soundless.

When we were in my room, I was about to sit on my bed when I stopped. I was afraid that sitting on the spring mattress would echo through the entire neighborhood.

I couldn't do anything but stand there in my wet clothes shivering. Jamie placed his arm around my shoulder and my body tensed. I was sure he'd noticed, but he didn't let go.

"It's going to be okay, Gwen," Jamie said softly in my ear. "They won't find us. Even if they do, we have the advantage in the darkness. We see them coming."

"We still only have knives."

The tears that started to leak out of the corners of my eyes were so warm it felt as though they were burning my cheeks. It felt like everything was crumbling down around me. Maybe it would have been better to have died with the rest of the world.

"I'm not going to let anything happen to you," Jamie said, squeezing me tighter.

"You won't be able to stop them," I said stepping away from him. I didn't want to hear his words. I lowered my voice softer than a whisper. "We need to be quiet. You should go."

Jamie shook his head. "I don't want to leave you alone."

"Go, Jamie," I said, my tone steady even though my lip quivered. "Leave."

He'd looked as though I'd punched him in the stomach, but he held up both hands. His eyes were glued to me as he backed out of my room. I could tell he was hoping I'd change my mind and ask him to stay.

Jamie didn't close the door behind him, but he walked out of view. The tears wouldn't stop, not even after I curled up on the floor and pressed my face into the pillow I'd pulled off of my bed.

Even though it was silent, I couldn't stop imagining the men storming into my apartment and coming into my bedroom. They looked down at me and all I could see with the big round circles filled with darkness where their eyes should have been.

I pulled my legs tight to my chest, hoping my tears would warm my wet, cold, shivering body. I was lost. It didn't feel like there was anything left I could do.

I just wanted everything to end. The sooner they came, the sooner it would be over.

There was a soft knock at the door, and a small gasp escaped from between my lips. A small part of me wondered if the men would be standing there, but then I realized they wouldn't knock.

I turned my head slightly and saw Bronx's shadow in my doorway. His hand dropped down from the door frame and fell heavily to his side.

He took a step into my room, both hands that had been clenched into tight fists, relaxed. "They're gone."

TWENTY-THREE

He knelt down on the ground next to me and let out a breath. I couldn't move, or maybe I just didn't have the energy to move.

"They left about ten minutes ago. It seemed as though they checked out a few more buildings before walking back through the yard. I think they gave up," Bronx said.

"Maybe for the night," I said, my voice lacking emotion.

Bronx reached out and lightly brushed away the icy tear that started to roll down my cheek. I could feel him staring at me through the darkness.

"Everything is going to be okay," Bronx said softly.

"I'm really getting sick of hearing that. Things

are already so far from okay it's not even funny," I muttered.

Bronx sighed. "Okay, you're right. But we'll figure this out. We'll get them back."

"If they're even still alive." It was my turn to sigh. "Maybe we should just go. I'd rather drown in the flood water than get shot in the head by one of those guys."

Bronx didn't say anything. He was probably trying to come up with a way to convince me that finding them was what we needed to do. If that was the case, he was struggling to find the words... not that there were any.

I shivered, and he touched my hand. "You're freezing."

"I fell into the water, remember?" My tone even annoyed me.

"We should probably get you changed," Bronx said getting to his feet. "Where can I find something for you to change into?"

I didn't answer. It was frustrating that I wanted him to leave me alone, but at the same time, I couldn't be alone.

"Let's see," he said peering at my dresser through the darkness. He pulled the t-shirt I had set down on the top of earlier and looked at it. "How about this?"

"Sure," I said without looking.

"Okay, well then, let's get you out of that soaking wet shirt," Bronx said, with a chuckle. "That sounds like a really bad pickup line, but trust me, I can barely see you in the dark."

I pushed myself up, but my body felt like it was made of ice. My bones were frozen stiff.

"It's fine," I said, my fingers stiff and shaky as I tried to grab the hem of my shirt. My arms were practically useless.

"Let me help," Bronx said moving behind me. He placed his hands on my arms and guided them over my head. I couldn't stop shivering as he pulled my wet shirt over my body and quickly replaced it with the dry one he'd found.

He pulled the blanket off of my bed and wrapped it around my shoulders easing me back to the floor.

"Why aren't you on the bed?" he asked as he moved down to my feet.

"It's too noisy," I said as he pulled off my shoes. "I should probably keep those on in case we need to run."

"Do you have a dry pair?" Bronx's hand slid up my leg and over my thigh.

His hand felt like a hot coal moving over my

frozen body. He popped the button of my pants with ease and wiggled them down my legs.

"In the closet," I said wrapping myself tighter in the blanket. "I'll worry about it later."

"I'd rather you had some just in case," Bronx said.

"How about pants first?"

He blew out a sharp breath between his lips. "Right. Where can I find a dry pair of those?"

"On the chair."

Bronx reached over and pulled the wrinkled up knit pants off of the chair near the dresser. I could feel his eyes on me as he slipped my feet inside the warm fabric.

"I got it," I said pulling away from him slightly.

In the darkness, I could see him raising both palms up in the air as he inched back.

"Sorry," he said quickly. "Was just trying to help."

"I know, and I appreciate it," I said putting my head back down on the pillow. "Thanks to you I can feel my fingers again."

"Of course, anything else I can do? I could stumble my way into the kitchen and find you something to eat," Bronx said looking over his shoulder. "Might help warm you up."

I shook my head even though he probably couldn't see the movement in the darkness. "No, thanks, I'm good."

"You sure? It's no trouble."

"Yeah, I'm not even a little hungry."

"Okay," he said moving closer to my head. "I'll let you get some rest then."

I wanted to laugh, but I figured I'd been rude enough for the day. It wasn't like I was going to be getting any sleep and even if I did, it wouldn't even come close to being restful.

"Sure," I said.

Bronx leaned over and kissed the top of my head. He hesitated for a moment before getting to his feet.

"I'll let you know if anything changes out there," Bronx said.

"Thanks."

"If you need anything, just let me know," Bronx said turning to leave the room before waiting for a response. He hadn't even given me the chance to tell him I could take care of myself.

Maybe he didn't think I could.

Maybe he was right.

I hadn't managed my life well before the attack, and it shouldn't have come as a surprise that I wouldn't be able to manage it after either. But that didn't mean I was just going to sit back and let everyone go out of their way to take care of me. I was starting to wonder if some of the things going through my mind, were the same things that had crossed Maggie's mind as she'd laid on the floor staring at the wall.

Then again, maybe what had gone through her mind had been completely different. For all I'd known, she'd managed her life perfectly right up until the attack.

Even though my body had warmed significantly, I shivered. I didn't want to be alone.

With my blanket wrapped around me, I made my way into the living room. Jamie was on the sofa, but his bright eyes cut through the darkness. Bronx was sitting near the window with his back to the wall. His eyes were closed, but I could tell by each breath he took that he was still awake.

"You okay?" Jamie asked peering at me through the blackness.

"Yes," I said my voice soft and raspy. "Didn't want to be alone."

"Don't blame you," Jamie said.

I laid down on the floor in the same spot my brother had claimed as his own. My eyes focused on the ceiling watching for glints of light that might pierce through the window and stab the walls.

The rain had slowed to a soft barely audible drizzle. In the distance, I could occasionally hear a soft rumble. It sounded like the storm was finally leaving which would hopefully mean that the flooding would soon recede. Not that we could wait for that to happen because I'm sure Nick and the others were living on borrowed time.

"We can try again tomorrow night," Bronx said, his voice floating through the air like smoke.

"What if they try again tomorrow?" Jamie said the exact same thing I was thinking.

"What if we set up a light in another apartment?" Bronx asked.

Jamie blew out a puff of air. "That won't work for long. They'll know we're in here somewhere."

"What if it's enough to distract them long enough that we can find where they're hiding our friends?" Bronx asked.

"Seems too risky," Jamie said.

There was a long pause. When neither of them spoke, I'd assumed they'd run out of ideas.

"Maybe they won't bother to check here again. If they did, that would suggest that they're suspicious,"

I said. "We could watch and see if they go out again tomorrow night."

"Or maybe I should go out on my own," Bronx said. "Hmm, yeah, I could look for them on my own, follow them."

"No," I said sitting up slightly. I wanted to look at him to see if he was serious.

Bronx hugged his knees to his chest. "It could be the best chance we have to find them."

"We can't lose you too," I said swallowing hard.

"You won't lose me. It's riskier for all of us to go. If it's just me—"

"No," I said sharply. "Just no."

Jamie shifted around. "Maybe it's not a terrible idea."

I turned my neck so fast I thought I gave myself whiplash. Jamie probably couldn't see me glaring at him, but I was.

"I know I can do it without being seen. Gwen," Bronx said getting to his feet, "this could be our only shot."

My head was shaking so rapidly I could feel my brain moving around in my skull. If I would have had any tears left, they would have been running down my cheeks. I fought off the sourness that was bubbling up in my stomach.

"You can't do this," I said my voice scratching the back of my throat.

"It'll be fine," Bronx said avoiding my eyes. "I'll be back before morning."

He glanced out the window before pulling on his shoes. They were still so wet they squished when he slipped his foot inside.

I walked over to him and placed my hand on his bicep. He looked down at my hand, holding his gaze for a moment before shifting his eyes to meet mine.

"Bronx," I whispered shaking my head. I wondered if he could see the fear in my eyes.

If he could, he ignored it. He stepped away from me and over to the counter, taking the flashlight in hand.

"I'll be back before you know it," Bronx said over his shoulder.

"Please don't go," I begged. I walked over to him and stood behind him, following him as he walked to the door. "Let's talk about this."

He looked out of the peephole, but surely he couldn't see anything. His fingers wrapped around the doorknob.

"There isn't anything to talk about." Bronx turned to the side. "I'll be back soon."

"Bronx! No!" I said doing my best to keep my

voice down. My fingers dug into the thick muscle of his arm.

Bronx opened the door and pulled away from me, stepping out into the hallway. He disappeared into the darkness.

TWENTY-FOUR

I took a step after him, but Jamie pulled me back into the apartment. He closed and locked the door before I could do anything... not that I knew what to do.

"It's going to be okay," Jamie said softly. "If anyone can do this, it's Bronx."

"Oh please," I groaned. "You're just happy he's out there and not you."

His jaw dropped down, stunned at my words. "Is that what you think of me?"

I couldn't respond. It wasn't Jamie's fault that Bronx was out there, he was just the closest target.

I walked over to the window and peered out of the small opening between the window frame and the curtain. Jamie stepped up to the other side of the window

"I would go out there if I had to," Jamie said after a long moment. There was still no sign of Bronx.

"I'm sorry," I said my voice below a whisper. "I shouldn't have said that."

"But you meant it."

I pressed my lips together and shook my head. "I didn't mean it. You don't see me out there, and it's my brother."

Several minutes passed. I could hear Jamie's soft breathing as I looked out the window searching for any signs of Bronx.

"Hey," I said lightly touching Jamie's arm and letting my hand fall back at my side.

"Yeah?"

"I really am sorry for saying that. It was awful, and I didn't mean it." I bit my lip when he didn't say anything. "I hope you can forgive me."

Jamie turned slightly and flashed me a half-grin. "Already have."

I smiled back, but it wasn't much of a smile. Not because I didn't mean it, but because I was worried sick and it was the best I could manage.

My words had already done their damage. Jamie

may have said he'd forgiven me, but I could tell what I'd said had still stung him.

"Where is he?" I muttered. It was odd that we hadn't seen him by now. He had to have made his way through the first floor and out the window... unless of course there had been some kind of hold up.

There hadn't been any ripples from movement or glints of light from his flashlight in the water.

"He's stealthy," Jamie said.

"Or something happened."

"If something would have happened, we would have seen something by now." Jamie placed his hand on the wall. "It's a good sign that we can't see him."

I shook my head. "Why?"

"Because if we can't see him neither can they."

Over what felt like hours, Jamie and I took turns staring out the window. Not once had either of us seen any sign of Bronx or anyone else for that matter.

My stomach was in knots with worry. What if something happened? What if he wouldn't come back? What if we lost all of them and it was only Jamie and I left?

The questions repeated in my head. Even when I was lying on the floor, squeezing my eyes shut, the questions didn't stop looping through my mind.

"You should try to get some rest," Jamie said, his voice cutting through the silence so sharply I jumped. "We don't know what tomorrow will hold."

"I don't think I can sleep." I swallowed hard. "At least not until he's back."

"Oh," Jamie said. "I see."

I couldn't see his expression through the darkness, but he sounded... hurt.

"It's just that I'm worried," I said sitting and hugging my legs to my chest. "Just as I would be if it were you out there."

"But not Nick? Blair?" Jamie cleared his throat. "Or Maggie?"

I looked down at my sock covered feet. I never did get my spare shoes.

"With Nick it's complicated, and I don't really know Blair or Maggie." I shook my head as I finished my sentence. "Of course, that doesn't mean I want anything to happen to them."

"Seems to me you didn't really know Bronx all that well either," Jamie said.

I opened my mouth but snapped it shut. He was right. I hadn't known him that much better than the others. Maybe I'd spent a little more time with him than Blair or Maggie, but not all that much.

There had been a connection with Bronx. I

didn't really know how to explain it. I wasn't even sure if I understood it.

"I guess not," I said with a shrug. "It's just stressful. Maybe it's all just getting to me."

I opened my mouth although I wasn't sure what I was going to say but luckily a soft tap on the door stopped my thoughts. Jamie and I locked eyes for a moment before he soundlessly moved across the floor.

He looked out of the peephole and looked at me over his shoulder. A smile curled up at the ends of his lips.

"He's back," Jamie said as he twisted the doorknob.

TWENTY-FIVE

Bronx stood near the door soaking wet. Droplets of water fell from the peaks of his drenched hair down onto the floor.

There was a touch of light on the walls from the sun that was just starting to rise. Bronx shivered, and looked up, meeting my eyes.

"I found them," Bronx said his voice hard.

"You did?" I said, my voice scratching my throat like sandpaper.

"I think so," Bronx said checking the lock on the door before kicking off his shoes. He shivered again before pulling off his shirt revealing his hard six-pack. "But it's not going to be easy to get to them."

I turned and walked into the bathroom, grabbing Bronx a towel. He nodded as he took it and dried himself off. Jamie and I exchanged a glance as we waited for Bronx to go on.

"They aren't far," Bronx said holding the towel in front of himself as he unbuttoned his pants, undressing in front of us as if it were no big deal. "There's a house, about two blocks away. The place was lit up with candles, but it wasn't just that, there were what appeared to be armed guards just inside the doors that gave it away."

Bronx wrapped the towel around his waist and picked up his wet clothes. He looked around the room trying to find a place to hang them.

"Here," I said holding out my hand.

"Thanks," he said, picking up one of the blankets off of the floor, the one I assumed was his, and wrapped it around himself before tossing me the towel.

The light in the room slowly increased. I could feel both of them watching as I draped his wet clothes over the backs of my dining room chairs. I awkwardly set his boxers down last and wrapped my arms around myself.

Bronx flashed me a half-grin before clearing his throat. "It's that big, red brick house on the corner. You guys know it?"

"Yeah," I said, and Jamie nodded.

"There's a front door, and a back door, but both appeared to be guarded. I couldn't even guess how many people were inside, but occasionally shadows would move by the window." Bronx sat down on the chair and raked his fingers through his hair. "I'm willing to bet there are more than just those three men we keep seeing."

"So, what do we do?" Jamie asked.

The light in the room was bright enough that we could see each other. Bronx pressed his fingertip into his forehead and shook his head.

"I'm too tired to think clearly," he said. "And I'm pretty sure my insides are at least half frozen."

"Get some sleep," I said hoping he didn't see the bags under my eyes. "We'll figure something out."

Bronx nodded. When he didn't argue, I knew he must have been exhausted.

"You should probably get some sleep too," Jamie said. "I'll stay up and keep a look out."

I tried to come up with an excuse, but when I opened my mouth, a yawn escaped instead of words.

"Go on," Jamie said. "Maybe they've given up on us."

"Maybe they don't even know there is an us," Bronx said lowering himself down to the floor. "That water is so cold I'm not sure they'll venture out more than they need to."

Jamie chewed his cheek. "If the rain ever stops and the sun comes out—"

"Wake me when that happens," Bronx said closing his eyes.

I turned to Jamie. "You need sleep too."

"It's fine," Jamie said. "I don't feel tired anyway."

"Yeah, right," I said with a soft chuckle.

"Go on," Jamie said.

I smiled and left the room. It was clear he wasn't going to take no for an answer, and I knew my body needed the rest. Of course, I didn't know if my mind was going to allow it. Maybe now that Bronx was back, it would.

I stared out of my bedroom window at the sky. The color had changed so drastically that I started to question if it had ever been as red as I remembered it in my mind.

The rain clouds hung low and moved slowly across the sky. The drizzle had turned into more of a sprinkle, but there wasn't a break in the clouds for as far as I could see.

I yawned again. This time so big it stretched the muscles in my neck.

The second my head hit the pillow I was out. I

wasn't sure if there was anything that could wake me.

* * *

Someone was moving around in the kitchen. I could tell by the soft noises they made that they were trying to be quiet, but with everything that was going on, I was even more of a light sleeper than I had been before.

I sat up and looked around. There was still some light coming in through the window but night would come soon. Several bones in my back cracked as I stretched my arms over my head.

I wrapped my arms around my middle as I made my way out of my room. A cold shiver ran down my spine not because I was frightened but because my body still hadn't warmed from when I'd been soaked.

Bronx was wearing only his boxers as he stood at the counter with his back to me. I could see the box of instant potatoes on the counter next to him. He turned sharply when the floorboard squeaked under my step.

"Oh," he said relaxing his broad, muscular shoulders, "did I wake you?"

"No, not really," I said glancing toward the sofa. Jamie appeared to be in a deep sleep.

"Good," Bronx said stirring the white slop vigorously. "I was trying to be quiet."

I pressed my lips together forming a tight curious smile. "I don't think that's going to work."

"What's that?"

"Your cold mashed potatoes."

Bronx shrugged. "I've had worse. Ever have pasta sauce made from ketchup?"

"I love ketchup."

Bronx chuckled softly and glanced over at the sofa before making eye contact with me. "So, I heard you were pretty worried about me?"

I blinked hard and then rolled my eyes. "Oh my God, what did he say?"

"Nothing much," Bronx said grinning so wide there were little wrinkles at the corners of his eyes. "Just that you couldn't sleep."

Bronx dipped the spoon into the bowl and raised the soupy potatoes to his lips. He held out the spoon and arched an eyebrow.

"No thanks," I said.

Bronx shrugged and slurped the mixture down. He cocked his head to the side, and continued to eat.

"I added too much water," Bronx said as he

walked around the counter and sat down at the table. "We're not going to be able to use the candles tonight. They'd be able to see the light through the curtains."

I nodded already assuming as much. Bronx moved the chair next to him out with his foot.

"Sit with me," he said softly.

I glanced over my shoulder at Jamie before sitting down. Bronx eyed me before shifting his gaze back to his bowl.

"My clothes are still wet," Bronx said jerking his chin toward his jeans. "Suppose you don't have spare clothes in my size, do you?"

I shook my head. "You're welcome to a pair of yoga pants if you'd like."

"They don't hug my curves right," Bronx said.

"Mine either," I said raising my brows quickly.

"I disagree." He set the spoon down in the bowl and leaned back in his chair. Bronx looked directly into my eyes. "I'm fairly certain you'd look good in anything."

Heat rose to my cheeks, and I hoped it was dark enough in the room that he hadn't noticed.

Bronx leaned forward, sliding his hand across the top of the table toward me. My heart started to pump heated blood through my veins quicker.

"All I could think about when I was out there, was coming back to you," Bronx said, his voice soft. "It killed me to walk away from you."

My voice seemed stuck in my throat. I pressed my fingertips to the center of my chest. "I shouldn't have done that."

"Done what?" Bronx asked cocking his head to the side.

"Asked you to stay like that."

He leaned forward again and took my hand into his. "I shouldn't have left... at least not like that." He shook his head and looked down at his feet. "I feel terrible about it. I don't want you to hate me."

"I don't hate you." I barely managed to get the words out. The air around us bubbled with an intensity I hadn't felt in a long time, if ever, and it made it hard for me to breathe. I was used to people leaving me, it wasn't like I should have expected any different from a man I barely knew.

Bronx slid forward to the edge of his chair. Our knees touched as he leaned in even closer.

My body shivered as he glided his hand up my arm, over my shoulder, and around my neck. Every nerve-ending tingled.

Bronx stared hungrily into my eyes as the light started to vanish from the room. He reached forward wrapping his hand around my waist and pulled me closer.

My breath hitched. Our faces were only inches apart. Looking into his dark eyes felt too intimate.

When my eyes moved down to his mouth, he moved quickly, as if he couldn't stand it any longer. He brushed his warm lips against mine and every muscle in my body tensed.

I felt weightless as our mouths danced together. Bronx's hand moved down my back, sliding me closer to him. I pressed my palm to his solid chest, and for a minute I forgot where I was.

Bronx's lips moved over my chin and down my neck. My head tipped back, and I had to bite back the moan that tried to escape between my slightly parted lips.

The sofa creaked, and my body stiffened. Bronx pulled back but didn't let go when Jamie let out a groan.

Bronx looked at me with a fire burning deep in his eyes. I let my hand fall away from his bare chest and forced myself to take a step away from him.

Jamie sat up, his back to us, as he stretched his arms over his head. He leaned forward and pressed his palms to his eyes.

"I don't want this to stop," Bronx whispered, his

breath touching my cheek. "I'm not sure I can walk away from you right now."

My heart pounded at his words. Maybe things were going too fast. I didn't want to walk away from him either, but I wasn't exactly sure how we ended up where we were.

Jamie turned around and peered at us through the darkness of the room. I could see that his eyes were narrowed as he looked at us.

"Is everything okay?" Jamie said, his voice scratchy.

"Yeah," Bronx said. "Everything is fine."

"Thank God." Jamie sighed. "It was just a bad dream."

Neither Bronx nor I asked what the dream had been about, and Jamie didn't tell us. I didn't even want to know.

I could still feel the heat radiating out of Bronx. Were we standing too close? I walked over to the window, and my body temperature seemed to drop by ten degrees.

"Well now that you're up, I suppose this is as good of a time as any," Bronx said.

"For?" Jamie asked.

Bronx let out a heavy breath. "To come up with our plan."

TWENTY-SIX

Jamie grabbed some snacks from the kitchen and sat down on the sofa. Bronx stepped up beside me. It felt like he was too close as he looked down into my eyes.

"Have a seat," he said gesturing to the chair.

I blinked, unable to stop thinking about what it had felt like to have his lips on mine. He lightly placed his hand on my lower back and guided me toward the chair near the window. The chair Nick had frequently sat in.

Nick.

Dammit.

I sat down, my back achingly stiff. My body wouldn't allow me to relax.

I swallowed as I turned to look at Bronx, waiting

for him to start the conversation. His eyes were narrowed as he looked out of the window, but then his head dropped before turning to face us.

Bronx slowly crossed his arms. "Well," he said rubbing his hands together, "the first thing we know is that we have to go at night. We're going to at least need the element of surprise."

"That's the first thing you want to do, surprise people that have assault rifles," Jamie said, sarcasm dripping from his tone.

"Do you have a better idea?" Bronx asked sharply.

Jamie was still for a long moment before looking away. "I guess I don't."

I sighed as I combed my fingers through my hair. My body relaxed only slightly as I drew in a deep breath.

There was a flash of light on the wall at the corner of the room, and I stood abruptly.

"Gwen?" Bronx said. I could feel his eyes on me.

My breaths quickened, and I started to feel light-headed. I blinked several times staring at the wall as if I expected to see the light again and have an explanation for it.

"Are you okay?" Jamie said as he stood.

"There was a light," I said pointing a shaky finger at the wall.

Bronx turned, his wide eyes staring out of the small space at the window. "Dammit!"

He dashed to the table and started to pull on his clothing. I stepped over and looked down at the yard. The light from their flashlights sparkled on the rippling water as they walked toward the apartment building.

"What are we going to do?" I said, my heart racing. There was only one way in and one way out... our options were limited.

"We could try hiding in another apartment," Jamie suggested.

Bronx shook his head. "That will only work for so long. Plus, it's too dark out there, and we don't know the condition of the other rooms, someone could get hurt. Shit!" he said between his teeth. "They're already inside."

"How much time do we have?" I asked as Bronx stepped away and started stuffing the backpacks into the already full closet.

"Not enough." Bronx grabbed me by the shoulders and looked into my eyes. "Put your shoes on and go hide at the back of your closet." His gaze hardened. "Do not come out no matter what. Promise?"

"No, of course not," I said my eyebrows squeezed together.

Bronx groaned and gave me a light push toward my room.

"What are you going to do?" I asked holding my breath when I thought I heard a noise. It sounded like they were in the stairwell, but I was only guessing.

Bronx patted his knife and raised a brow. "I'll be waiting for them."

"That isn't going to help you," I said feeling the moisture leave my mouth.

Bronx placed his hand on Jamie's shoulder. "Find somewhere to hide."

Jamie nodded and grabbed the blanket he'd been using. He curled up behind the chair pulling the blanket over himself. In the darkness, he practically disappeared.

Bronx grabbed my hand and dragged me through the apartment, picking up my shoes that were still probably wet as we walked by.

"The candles!" I said. Even though they weren't lit, having them out was a big neon sign.

"I'll take care of it," Bronx said opening the closet door in my bedroom. He kissed me hard, but it only lasted a second. "Do not come out."

Bronx soundlessly closed the closet door and walked away. I heard a few noises like he was moving things... hiding things... and then complete silence. All I could hear was the sounds of my breathing and my quickened heartbeat.

Random thoughts zipped through my head. Maybe it was my life flashing before my eyes. A memory of Nick and I playing with play-doh as kids popped in with a blink. My mom smiling at me as she rocked in her chair during her soap opera. But all the memories poofed away when I heard the men at the door.

They were here.

We were screwed.

TWENTY-SEVEN

The knob squeaked and rattled as they tried to get in. There were a few mumbles before something slammed hard into the door. I shuddered and covered my mouth.

My closet was pitch black. I couldn't see anything, but I could feel my clothing hanging all around me.

Shivers ran through my body. Even though I knew I was alone in the closet, it didn't feel that way. It felt like there were hands inches from touching me. Eyes that I knew were really there stared at me... mouths of the invisible hanging agape.

It took the men several tries, but it wasn't long before I heard the cheap wooden door crack. They were talking to one another, but their voices were muffled by what I could only assume was their masks... and of course my closet door.

"This is the one," one of the men said, at least that's what I thought he said.

I could hear them moving around my apartment, not even trying to be quiet. They'd come right to my room. Had they known we were here?

"Looks like they're gone," a different man said. He was close. And when his light flashed under the closet door, I knew he was really close. "Bedroom's empty."

"They're not gone," the first man said. My blood ran cold as something slammed down hard. "Trash is full."

"That don't mean anything," the third man said.

The first man chuckled. "Maybe not but I don't think they would have left all this water behind, do you?" He slammed the refrigerator door closed, and for a second I thought my heart had stopped. "Not to mention their fear smells stronger than the trash. They want to play hide and seek with us."

"Come out, come out wherever you are," one of the men said, and the other two laughed.

There was a scuffle nearby... the bathroom? Then a stream of curses.

"Here's one, dad," one of the men said.

"Told you not to call me that."

"Shit sorry, boss," the man said. "This one was doing a shitty job hiding in the bathroom."

Bronx. It had to be Bronx. My stomach started to swirl so wildly I was afraid something was going to come up.

"Tie him up," the one I now knew was the dad said. "How many more of you are there in here?"

"It's just me," Bronx said, the tone of his voice rough and filled with anger.

"That's not what she said," one of the men said.

There was a loud slapping noise... it sounded as if something had been hit. My eyes widened as I placed my hand over my mouth.

"Relax your muscles," the one they'd called dad shouted.

"They are," Bronx spat.

The floorboards in my room started to squeak, and I froze. If the other two men were talking to Bronx, I couldn't hear it. The only thing I could hear was the noises of a stranger walking through my room.

From time to time the light touched the cracks of the door. I wasn't sure if the clothing and random items in front of me hid me well enough from view.

"Ah ha!" the man said, but when the door didn't

open, and my bed springs squeaked, I realized he was looking under the blankets. "Oooookay," he sang, his voice was low but squeaking with excitement, "I know you're in here."

The closet door jerked open and the light shined into the closet. I caught a glimpse of the round clear lenses of his gas mask that mostly hid his eyes. It didn't seem as though he saw me.

I pressed my hand down harder against my mouth when he shifted the clothing to my left to the side.

"Boo!" he said, but clearly, he hadn't found me. The light from his flashlight lit up his dripping-wet, mud-covered shoes. The man took a step back leaving a footprint on the carpet. He started to close the door, but before it clicked closed, he abruptly pulled it open wider and pushed the clothing in front of my face to the side. "Peek-a-boo!"

"No!" I said taking a step back, but the wall stopped me from escaping. The barrel of his gun was pointed at my nose from just inches away.

"Out!" he said, but when I didn't move, he raised his voice. "Get! Out!"

I stepped out, wrapping my arms around myself. Every inch of my body trembled, and I wasn't sure if I was hiding it.

"Found another," the guy behind me said poking the gun in my back.

"Well tie her up," the one they called dad said.

The third guy grabbed a chair from the table and set it next to where Bronx was. Every so often the light from their flashlights skimmed across his face. I could see the worry in his eyes, but his face was filled with anger.

"If you hurt her," Bronx growled.

"Shut up," the dad said raising his gun. He flashed his light at Bronx and then at me just as his sons finished tying me to my chair. "Any more of you hiding in here?"

I shook my head. "It's just us."

He studied my face. I did everything I could to hold it in place because I knew that Jamie was still hiding under the blanket behind the chair. And he might be our only chance at making it out alive.

"I thought she said there were three?" one of the men said.

"He left," Bronx said. "He went out looking for our friends and never came back."

"We looked everywhere, boss. I think he's telling the truth," the taller of the two men said.

The dad cocked his head to the side. "Let's be safe. Check everything again."

The dad pulled up a chair and sat several feet in front of Bronx and me. He crossed his legs and rested his gun across his lap.

"So, we're going to have a little chat before I drag your asses out of here." There was enough light that I could see the man pull out a pack of cigarettes from the front pocket of his coat. He tapped one out and placed the tip just inside his mouth. He clicked the lighter, and the end glowed in the darkness, lighting his face when he inhaled. "Tell me what you know about the red sky."

Bronx looked over at me and our eyes locked. His eyes were about as wide as mine felt.

"You tell us," Bronx said shaking his head.

The man chuckled as his sons walked around and stood behind him holding their guns across their chest. He pointed to his gas mask.

"We have to wear these, you don't. I think you know more than you're letting on," the man said. "It took a while to get your friends to talk, and now one of them is dead. Hopefully, you two won't be as difficult."

Dead? Nick?

"We aren't going to be difficult," Bronx said his shoulders rising up toward his ears. "We don't know anything."

"Your friend told us about you, and about this place. They withstood a lot before she broke down," the man said uncrossing his legs and leaning forward. "I should warn you, it's been a rough few days, and I'm not feeling very kind tonight."

I swallowed hard. Had Blair talked? Maggie?

"What did she tell you?" I said softly.

"You tell me first what you know."

I bit my lip. "I woke up, and the sky was red, that's all I know."

"Bull shit." The man stood and took two steps until he was standing directly in front of Bronx. "How are you able to breathe the air? Everyone else got sick. Did they give you a shot? Some kind of vaccine?"

Oh my god. The guy was insane. We were in more trouble than I'd even realized.

"I didn't get a shot." My head was shaking from side to side vigorously.

"Me either," Bronx said. "We're just as in the dark as you are about all of this."

The man laughed but stopped abruptly. Darkness filled his eyes as he raised his fist and threw into the side of Bronx's face.

Bronx's head drooped down and rocked slicked before he straightened himself. The man put his flashlight several inches from Bronx's face. Blood trickled out of a small cut on the side of his lip as he narrowed his eyes to avoid the light.

"Lies," the man said.

What had either Blair or Maggie told the men?

Bronx's jaw stiffened. The man pulled the light back quickly, and I couldn't see Bronx's face any longer, but I could hear his groan.

"Okay, I can see we're going to have to do this the hard way," the man said placing his hands on his hips. "So, everyone got sick at the same time, the sky was red, my family," he said clearing his throat. It looked like he'd wished he would have chosen his words better. "My people had to wear these masks, so we didn't get sick. Thank goodness we were prepared. But here's the weird thing, there are people out there like you and your friends, that didn't get sick and die."

"I got sick," I said.

The man stared at me hard. He raised his hand and slapped me across the face.

I closed my eyes. Through the prickles of where I'd been hit I could hear Bronx's chair moving across the floor.

"I'll kill you!" Bronx spat. "What kind of man raises his hand to a woman? Tied up no less."

Out of the corner of my eye, I saw the man raise his foot. He threw enough force behind the kick to Bronx's face that it knocked the whole chair backward.

"Bronx!" I shouted!

"Bronx? What the fuck kind of name is that?" the man said looking over his shoulder at one of his sons. They both laughed as if cued. "I can see these stupid fuckers aren't going to talk. We'll have to do to them what we did to their friends."

The man walked over to Bronx while one of his sons turned my chair. He grabbed my head and forced me to look down at them while the other pointed his flashlight at them.

"Leave him alone," I cried, but that just made them laugh more.

The man placed his foot on Bronx's head and pushed it down flat against the ground. He turned up to me, and all I could see was blackness in his eyes.

"Are you going to talk or am I going to have to crush his skull?" the dad asked.

"What do you want to know?" I said trying to sound as though I was going to cooperate. The only problem was I had no idea what to say, and I was afraid that no matter what I said, it would be the wrong thing. I now understood why either Blair or Maggie had talked.

"I want to know what they gave you... the vaccine or the antidote or whatever it was," the man said.

I shook my head trying to stop the tear that leaked out of the corner of my eye. "There was no drug. We all got sick!"

Bronx gritted his teeth as the man pushed down harder.

"Are you sure about that?" the man asked.

"Okay, okay! Stop! There was a medication," I screamed.

"I knew it!" the man said lifting his foot only slightly. "Did you work for whoever was behind this?"

I shook my head, but then his grimace quickly changed it to a nod. My stomach was in knots.

"Do you have the drug here?" the man asked.

I had to do whatever I could to get him to release Bronx.

"Yes!" I said shaking as I noticed Jamie's wide eye peeking out from behind the blanket. He was less than four feet away from Bronx and the man. "It's in the bathroom. Let me show you."

Jamie's eye widened further.

"Where is it?" the man asked.

"Take me into the bathroom, and I'll get it for you," I said.

"You think I was born yesterday?" the man said. "Describe it."

I tried to think of what I had in my medicine cabinet that wouldn't obviously be pain medication. The only thing I could think of was what I'd been prescribed after my mom died.

"It's the only one in there. Brown bottle. White top," I said between sharp breaths. The second the man saw the drug listed on the label he'd slam his foot down on Bronx's head.

I had to do something. And fast.

TWENTY-EIGHT

The man that had been standing behind me walked away and into the bathroom. I could hear him moving things around in my medicine cabinet.

"Brown bottle," I shouted and both the man and his son turned to look at me. Both of their guns were down, but it looked like Bronx was about to lose consciousness.

"All I see is headache medicine, and that same anti-depressant mom has," the son called out.

Shit.

I forced a smile, but the dad was glaring at me. He jerked his head, and his son took a step forward and aimed his gun at the side of my head.

"It's in there," I said holding my smile. "Unless my brother stole it when he was here."

The two men exchanged a glance.

"She's lying," the dad said jerking his chin again.

His son lowered his gun and grinned before slamming his closed fist into my face near my eye. Pain pounded through my skull giving me an instant headache and blurring the vision in my left eye.

I winced just as Jamie launched himself out of his hiding spot and into the man in charge. They fell to the ground, rolling and rocking as Jamie tried to get on top.

"Shoot him!" the man yelled.

I kicked my leg up knocking the gun out of his son's hands.

"Bitch!" the son said bending down to pick up the gun. I kicked him as hard as I could with both of my legs.

"Stop!" the other son shouted as he stepped out of the bathroom. His gun pointed at Jamie. Before I could raise my foot again, the other son had his gun back against the side of my head.

I couldn't tell if Bronx was conscious or not. The darkness and my blurred vision was making it even harder to see even with the occasional flashes of light from their flashlights.

"Okay, okay!" Jamie said climbing off of the dad.

"Kill him!" the dad screeched backing away. His gun wasn't in his hand. "Kill them they're all liars! They're contaminated! He touched me! He was on top of me! Kill them!"

My eyes scanned the floor looking for the gun. Not that I could do anything about it with my hands tied up... and even if I could find it, I wouldn't have any idea how to use it.

"Let me think!" the son that had come out of the bathroom said. His gun inching closer to the space between Jamie's eyes.

His finger trembled.

"Pull it Danny!" his brother said.

"I haven't done this before," Danny said, his voice shaking.

"And you don't have to do it now," Jamie said.

Danny grimaced, and Jamie held up his hands.

"Give me your fucking gun, Dan," the dad demanded. "Enough of this shit."

Just as Dan reached over to hand the gun to his dad, my front door flung open. Nick was standing there, his face bruised and bloodied. His shirt and hands were covered in blood.

Blair was behind him just as bruised and bloodied, she looked smaller.

Nick was holding a gun just like the ones the men had, but in his right hand, he held his pistol. Blair was holding her very own gun but kept hers down at her side.

Nick's eyes quickly scanned the area. He didn't hesitate to put a bullet into the man at my side. Blood splattered onto my face, and the guy dropped to the floor.

"No!" dad cried out.

Before he could pull the gun away from his other son, another bullet ripped through the air. Blood pooled out of the hole in the dad's forehead.

"Don't shoot! Please!" Danny said stepping back toward the bathroom with his hands in the air.

Nick stared at him.

"Are you the one that shot my friend?" Nick asked.

"No," Danny answered quickly. "That was Ron. I've never even killed a fly. At least not on purpose."

"Untie them," Nick said over his shoulder.

Blair's entire body seemed to shake as she stepped into the apartment. She pulled one of the steak knives out of the drawer and walked over to me, looking into my eyes for a second before she started sawing at the rope.

"Jamie, pick up the guns... bring them to me,"

Nick ordered, and Jamie promptly obeyed. "Is he okay?"

Jamie shook his head.

I stood as the rope fell away, rubbing my wrists as I walked over to Bronx and dropped to my knees.

"Bronx?" I said shaking him.

He groaned. "Yeah."

"He's alive," I said over my shoulder, and Nick slammed the door shut and locked it.

"Use that rope, and tie up our new friend, Danny boy here," Nick said.

Danny's eyebrows drooped. "What are you going to do to me? Whose blood is that on your shirt?"

"Your mom's," Nick said curling his lip up at one end. "And this, over here," Nick said pointing at the other side of his shirt, "is your sister's."

Danny's shoulders started to shake, and his head fell down. He didn't struggle as Jamie and Blair tied him to the chair.

I was working my fingers quickly to untie Bronx. Nick knelt down beside me with the steak knife in hand.

"Let me," he said quickly sawing Bronx free.

I wrapped my arms around Bronx's weak body and tried to lift him. I sniffed, and Nick placed his hand on my shoulder for a moment before helping me get Bronx to the sofa.

"I'm okay," Bronx said sounding intoxicated. He waved his hands at us as he rested his head back. "The room is spinning."

The flashlights strewn about gave enough light that I could see Nick was staring at me.

"Are you okay?" Nick asked after a long moment. His fingertips moved up toward my eye, but he quickly pulled them back.

"Yeah, I'm okay."

"My head is killing me," Bronx said.

"That's because he was standing on it," I said resting my hand on his thigh. I looked back at Nick. "What happened out there?"

Nick shook his head. "Nothing good. They killed Maggie. Crazy fucking family."

Blair walked over to the chair. Her body moved stiffly... awkwardly as she lowered herself down.

"They tortured us," Nick said, and Blair looked away. Nick looked over at Danny. "The stupid fucks thought we were somehow involved in all this. Demanded we tell them what was going on."

"I'm sorry I told them about you," Blair said. "They were going to kill Nick. I couldn't have his blood on my hands too."

Blair looked down at the blood on her hands. The blood that belonged to the crazy family, but something told me she wasn't seeing their blood, she was seeing Maggie's.

"It's not your fault," I said.

"I should have lied," Blair said shaking her head. "But they were going to kill us both if they came back empty-handed. I needed to buy us some time."

"Bronx went out there... he saw where you were being held," I said.

Nick looked over at Bronx seemingly impressed. Bronx's eyes were a little wider, and he seemed to be coming back from wherever he'd gone.

"How did you get free?" I asked.

"With the three of them gone, it wasn't too hard. The other times they left we didn't know when they'd be back, we had to hope that this time we had more time." Nick said scratching the back of his neck. "We were tied up just like you."

Nick held up his hands, and even in the darkness I could see the raw, cut up flesh.

"Blair managed to wiggle free a day or two ago after they... they...," Nick's said his words fading.

"After they beat me," Blair said. "They didn't tie me up very good." Her chin jerked toward Danny. "He's not very good at tying."

Danny sniffed hard. His cheeks were red and tear-streaked. "I'm not good at anything. If you hadn't murdered my dad, he would have told you that himself."

"After she got me free, we did what we had to do to get back here," Nick said, pressing his lips tightly together.

"I'm glad you're back," I said. If he hadn't come back when he did, Bronx, Jamie, and I would probably be the ones lying on the floor... dead.

"I'm glad to be back," Nick said with a small smile. He stood and slapped his palms on his thighs. "I'm starving."

I stood and waved my hand at him. "Sit, let me get you something."

"If you insist." Nick shrugged and sat back down.

"Can I get you anything, Blair?" I turned to her. She still seemed to be shaking.

"Sure." Her head turned to the side. "But what are we going to do about him?"

I shook my head and turned back to Nick. I didn't even know what to do about the dead bodies on my apartment floor. It sort of felt as though I was in a dream... rather, a nightmare.

"Oh God," Danny said. "Please don't kill me."

"I promise nothing," Nick said. "I'll have to sleep on it."

When I stepped into the kitchen, I couldn't help but look over my shoulder to make sure someone wasn't standing behind me with a gun pointed at the back of my head. I jumped when Jamie stepped up next to me.

He reached his hand up and lightly touched the skin just under my eye. "It's swelling."

"I can't see clearly out of it," I said repeatedly blinking as if that would help.

"I should have acted faster," Jamie said letting his hand fall to his side. "If I would have done something sooner, it wouldn't have happened."

I shook my head. "You don't know that maybe something worse would have happened. Maybe we wouldn't even be standing here right now."

I looked up and noticed there was a touch of light peeking through the curtain. It would be morning soon.

Out of the corner of my eye, I saw Danny watching us. When I turned, he quickly looked away. He didn't look like he could have been a day over twenty.

Poor kid.

Nick stepped in front of me blocking my view of

Danny. He grabbed the snack bar from my hand and devoured it in two bites.

"How much food do we have left?" Nick asked.

"Still what we have in the bags, but not much." I crossed my arms. "I'm sure we can find more in some of the other apartments."

"Lots of stuff at Danny's place. Well, something to worry about for another day," Nick said nodding at Jamie. "Help me move their bodies?"

Jamie nodded and followed Nick over to the first body. Danny's brother. He lowered his head and started sobbing.

I watched them as they dragged the body out of the door and into the hallway. Blair stared at her feet, and Bronx turned, looking at me over his shoulder. His face was swelling more and more by the minute.

I turned toward the freezer to grab an ice pack but stopped. There was no ice. The only thing I could do to help Bronx was to offer him some pain relievers.

As I walked toward the bathroom, I noticed the light at the curtain was brighter than it had been. Bronx followed my gaze and walked over to the window. He pulled it to the side so I could see the bright sun.

I smiled, and he smiled back. The only thing I

was going to allow myself to think about was that it was a good sign. We would figure things out. We would be okay.

TWENTY-NINE

It had been several days, and things were still blurry. When I blinked, for a second, things seemed clear, but they'd quickly blur right back out.

The swelling in Bronx's face had mostly subsided, but the bruises were still visible. Nick and Blair were healing as well... at least physically.

Blair didn't talk much. Mostly she looked as though she was in a perpetual state of shock. The only time she was animated was when Nick was next to her whispering into her ear.

It was clear they'd been through hell. I didn't ask. None of us did. If they wanted to talk, they would in their own time, and maybe I didn't even want to know.

The rain had stopped, but some of the flooding

remained. I frequently checked out the window, hoping it would have receded, but it hadn't. Debris and the occasional pale body bobbed up and down as the water pulled them around the corner of the apartment.

Nick and Jamie had scrounged through some of the other apartments and found more food, but our water was running low. We were going to have to go, but even Nick seemed to want to wait until we had to. Maybe for Blair. Maybe for himself.

I couldn't blame them for not wanting to go back out there. The idea was nearly terrifying. But I couldn't let myself go there. I couldn't let myself think about it.

Besides, after what had happened, it only made me want to get to my grandma quicker. If she was still alive.

"Hey," Bronx said knocking lightly on my bedroom door.

"Hi," I said smiling at him.

He closed the door slightly as he stepped inside my room. "Thought you were sleeping."

I shook my head and stepped away from the window. I tried not to frown at the small, nearly healed cut on his lip.

Until the cuts, scrapes, and bruises were gone, I

wouldn't be able to forget. Who was I kidding? I wouldn't ever be able to forget... the injuries and my blurry vision were a constant reminder.

"Danny's been crying to come out," Bronx said.

"Again?"

"Nick let him out. Set him up near the window," Bronx said. "He's just a kid, but I just couldn't be in the same room as him... not right now."

I swallowed hard as he took a step closer. He slid his hand around the back of my neck.

"And I wanted to check on you," he said, his voice rumbled through my body. "I hate when you're out of sight."

Bronx pulled me closer and pressed his lips to mine. I kept my eyes closed as he pulled away, not wanting the moment to end.

"Nick wants to talk to us," Bronx said letting his hand slide down my arm until he reached my hand. He entwined his fingers with mine.

"He's ready?" I asked.

"Him and Blair both are." Bronx lowered his head, so he was looking directly into my eyes. "Are you?"

I chewed my cheek for only a second. "I am. You?"

"Yeah, as ready as I'll ever be." Bronx smiled so

wide I worried he'd open the cut on his lip. "Still don't know what to do about the kid."

"Not much we can do." I shrugged.

"By that you mean...?"

I narrowed my eyes at him. "Bringing him with us."

"We could just let him go," Bronx said.

"Alone? He's just a kid," I said hating that I didn't want to send him away. Hating that I cared what happened to him. "I know I sound crazy after what he and his family did to all of us."

Bronx squeezed my hand. "I'm not sure he did all that much."

"He didn't stop them. He didn't speak up."

"For all we know, he tried," Bronx said stepping to the side to peer out the window. "That bastard probably did everything he could to make sure his sons stayed in line."

"You sound just as conflicted as I feel," I said crossing my arms as I walked toward the door. I peeked out of the opening into the other room, but I couldn't see anything. I couldn't even hear anything.

Bronx stepped up next to me and nodded. "You ready to do this?"

"I guess."

Bronx followed me into the living room. Nick

stood and hauled Danny into the bathroom while he begged him to stop.

"Please! Don't lock me in there again!" he shouted. "I'm not doing anything wrong!"

"We just need some privacy," Nick said before slamming the bathroom door. He brushed his hands together as if he'd just finished weeding the garden. "Shall we have a seat?"

I sat down on the sofa, Bronx was to my left and Jamie to my right. Blair was curled up in the chair, staring at Nick who was standing in the middle of the room.

It was strange how we were all sitting in my living room like this again. Nick leading the conversation. A lot of things had changed since the last time we'd all been together like this.

"It's time to talk about when we leave," Nick said rubbing his hands together. "The water is slowly receding. I measured yesterday, it's roughly six inches deep, and very likely once we get to higher ground we won't even have to worry about it."

Nick paced one way, and then the other before stopping to face us again. It seemed like he was trying hard to convince us, but I wasn't sure that any of us needed convincing.

"We can double check the packs, and whatever

else we need we'll have to find out there. Our water supplies are low. I think it's time," Nick said.

"I think we're ready," Bronx said. "I'm sick of looking at the bloodstained carpet."

I nodded.

Nick turned to Blair.

"I'm with you," she said chewing her fingernail as she looked up into his eyes. "Whatever you want to do."

Nick turned to Jamie and Jamie offered him a small nod.

"Okay," Nick smiled. "Tomorrow? Now?"

"Tomorrow," I said. I wanted just one more night in my bed because I probably wasn't ever going to see it again. Was it weird how I was going to miss my bed?

"Tomorrow," Nick echoed. He let out a heavy sigh as he crossed his arms across his chest. "There is just one more thing we need to talk about."

I cocked my head to the side.

"What's that?" Jamie asked.

"Danny," Bronx said before Nick could respond.

Nick's head bobbed up and down as he pointed at Bronx. "That's exactly right. Danny."

"I don't care what happens to Danny," Blair said. "I think we should throw Danny out the window."

"No!" Danny shouted as the chair thumped against the tiled bathroom floor.

Nick stormed across the floor and slammed his fist into the bathroom door so hard I thought his hand was going to go right through the wood.

"You don't get a vote," Nick shouted.

"I should get a vote," Danny said, his voice mostly muffled by the door.

I stood up and turned to face Nick. "He's just a kid. He didn't do anything to us." I bit my lip. "Did he do anything to you?"

"No," Nick answered with a stiff jaw. "But we can't trust him."

"Yes, you can!" Danny shouted.

Nick rolled his eyes at the door. "Our other option is to let him go. Let him fend for himself."

"That's fine," Blair said as if it had been decided.

Nick looked at me as if waiting for my call. The problem was, I didn't know what call to make.

"Whatever you decide," I said. I exhaled as I looked at Bronx and Jamie. They both stared up at me wearing the same blank expression. I narrowed my eyes at them, something a bit too close to a scowl. "What?"

"Nothing," Bronx said shaking his head.

Jamie looked away.

I walked across the room and stood in front of Nick. "You shouldn't kill him."

"Thank you," Danny said sounding as if he'd been crying.

"That doesn't mean I won't," Nick said pounding his fist into the door again.

I leaned closer to Nick and lowered my voice. "Stop scaring him."

"He deserves to be scared." I started to walk toward my room, but Nick grabbed my arm. "You ready for this?"

I hesitated. My mouth curled up into a smile.

"I am," I said sounding surer about the decision than I ever had about anything in my entire life. And I was sure. After a good night's rest, I was ready to leave this apartment behind. I was ready to leave the whole city behind.

I wasn't excited to walk seventy-five miles to my grandma's, but we'd get there. If there was anyone that could do it, it was us.

We'd gotten through hell, and it was time... it was time to leave it behind. If there was help out there, eventually they'd find us. It didn't matter where we were as long as we were together.

BOOKS BY KELLEE L. GREENE

Falling Darkness Series

Unholy - Book 1

Uprising - Book 2

Hunted - Book 3

Ravaged Land Series

Ravaged Land -Book 1

Finding Home - Book 2

Crashing Down - Book 3

Running Away - Book 4

Escaping Fear - Book 5

Fighting Back - Book 6

Ravaged Land: Divided Series

The Last Disaster - Book 1

The Last Remnants - Book 2

The Last Struggle - Book 3

The Island Series

MAILING LIST

Sign up for Kellee L. Greene's mailing list for new releases, sales, cover reveals and more!

Sign up: http://eepurl.com/bJLmrL

You can Find Kellee on Facebook:

www.facebook.com/kelleelgreene

ABOUT THE AUTHOR

Kellee L. Greene is a stay-at-home-mom to two super awesome and wonderfully sassy children. She loves to read, draw and spend time with her family when she's not writing. Writing and having people read her books has been a long time dream of hers and she's excited to write more. Her favorites genres are Fantasy and Sci-fi. Kellee lives in Wisconsin with her husband, two kids and two cats.

For more information:
www.kelleelgreene.com

facebook.com/kelleelgreene

twitter.com/kelleelgreene

Made in the USA
Monee, IL
15 April 2023

31916930R00163